DC

TEEN TITANS GO!™

PARTY, PARTY
AND SILICON VALLEY CYBORG

Teen Titans Go! is published by
Stone Arch Books,
A Capstone Imprint
1710 Roe Crest Drive
North Mankato, MN 56003
www.mycapstonepub.com

Library of Congress Cataloging-in-Publication Data is available at the Library of Congress website:
ISBN: 978-1-4965-7995-9 (library binding)
ISBN: 978-1-4965-8001-6 (eBook PDF)

Summary: We all know the Teen Titans are great at throwing "hat parties" and "meatball parties" . . . but can they
throw a regular ol' "party party?" Don't miss who's on the guest list! Then when Cyborg is named CEO of the Silicon
Valley startup ChirpFolio, he hires the Titans as his first employees! Cyborg is out to show the world that ChirpFolio
is the next big thing! But . . . what is it that this company does, anyway?

Alex Antone Editor – Original Series Paul Santos Editor

STONE ARCH BOOKS
Chris Harbo Editor
Brann Garvey Designer
Hilary Wacholz Art Director
Kathy McColley Production Specialist

TEEN TITANS GO!

AMY WOLFRAM   RICARDO SANCHEZ
WRITERS

JORGE CORONA   BEN BATES
ARTISTS

JEREMY LAWSON
COLORIST

WES ABBOTT
LETTERER

DAN HIPP
COVER ARTIST

STONE ARCH BOOKS
a capstone imprint

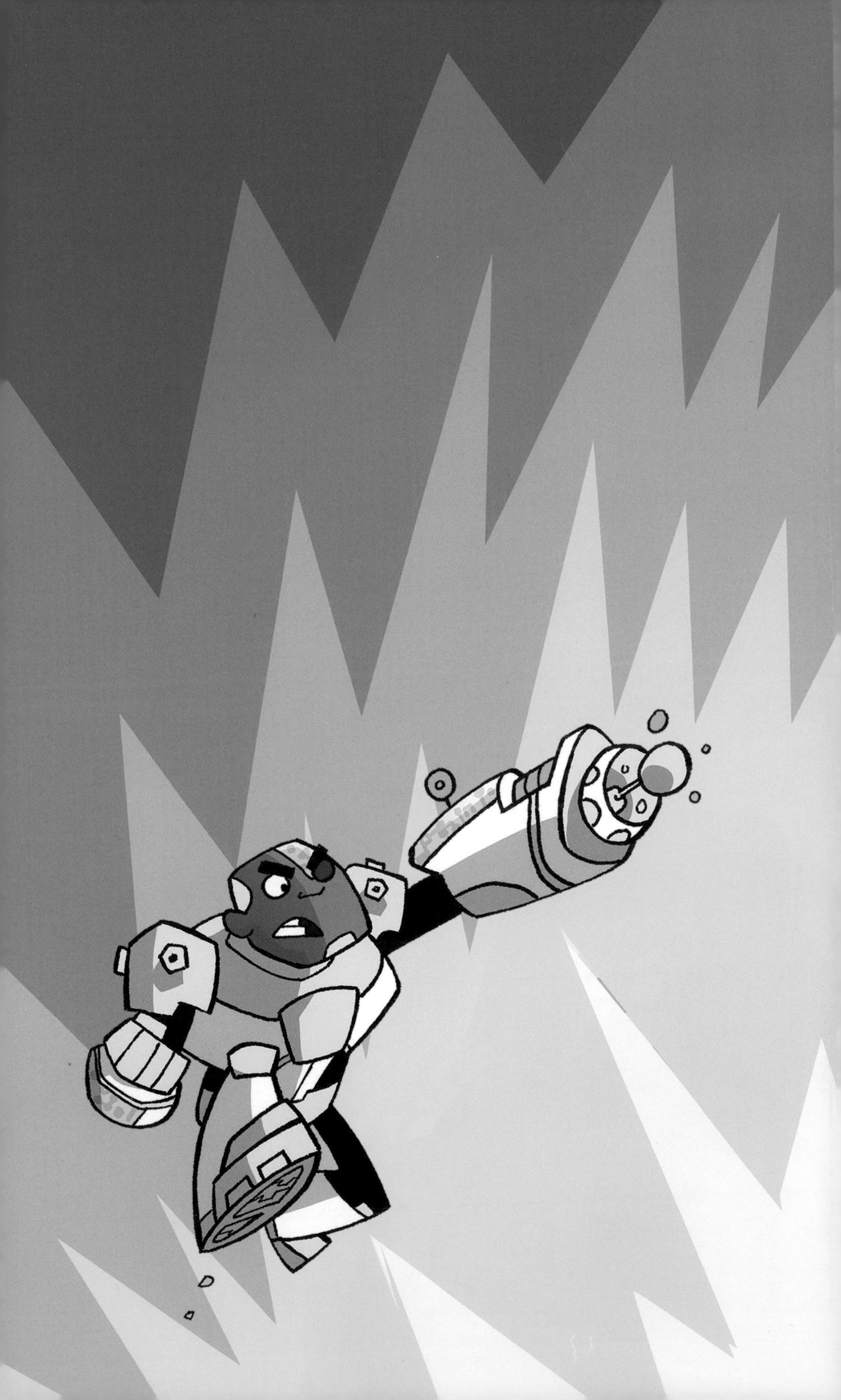

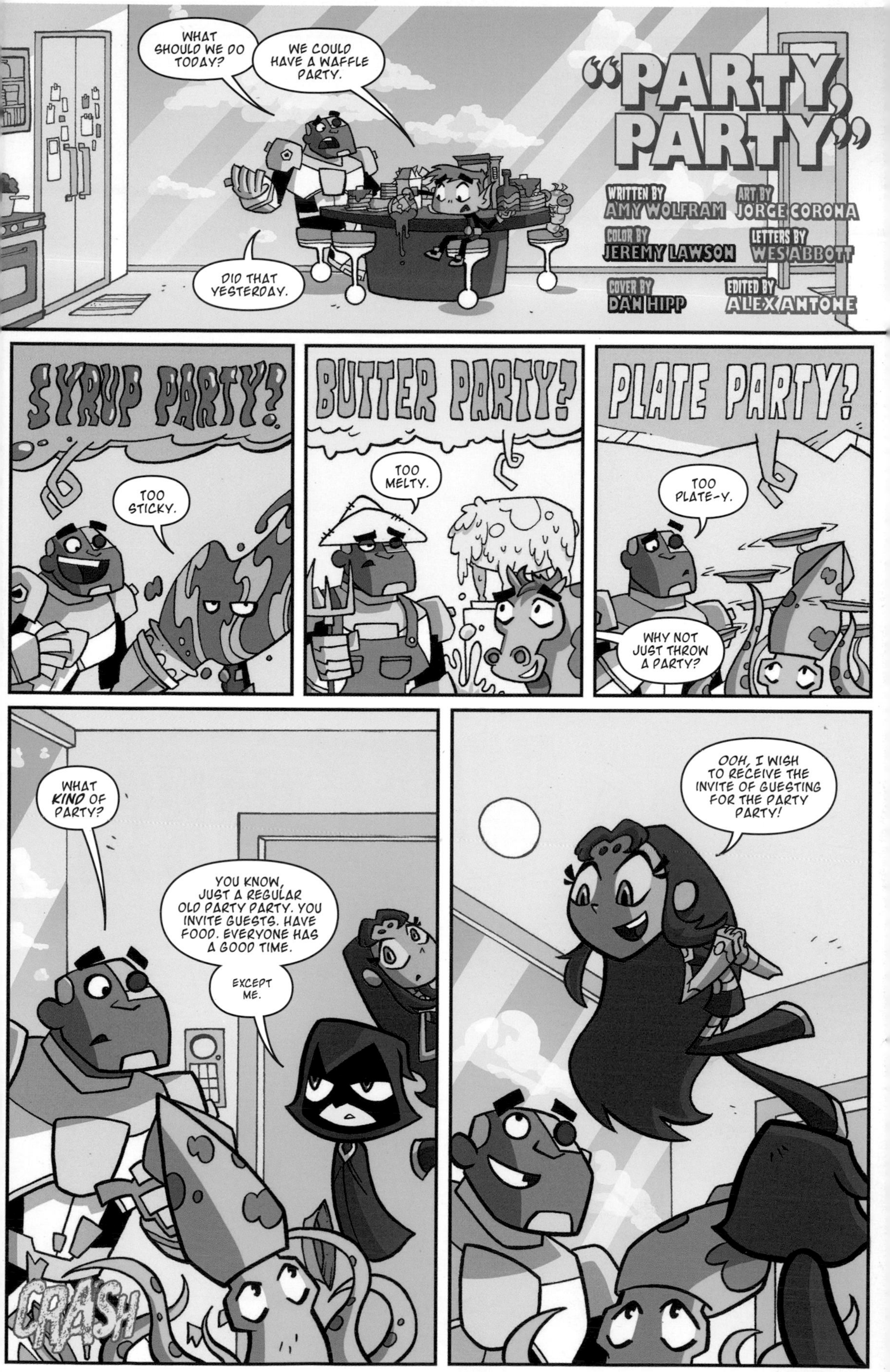
WHAT SHOULD WE DO TODAY?
WE COULD HAVE A WAFFLE PARTY.
DID THAT YESTERDAY.
"PARTY, PARTY"
WRITTEN BY AMY WOLFRAM
ART BY JORGE CORONA
COLOR BY JEREMY LAWSON
LETTERS BY WES ABBOTT
COVER BY DAN HIPP
EDITED BY ALEX ANTONE
SYRUP PARTY?
TOO STICKY.
BUTTER PARTY?
TOO MELTY.
PLATE PARTY?
TOO PLATE-Y.
WHY NOT JUST THROW A PARTY?
WHAT KIND OF PARTY?
YOU KNOW, JUST A REGULAR OLD PARTY PARTY. YOU INVITE GUESTS. HAVE FOOD. EVERYONE HAS A GOOD TIME.
EXCEPT ME.
CRASH
OOH, I WISH TO RECEIVE THE INVITE OF GUESTING FOR THE PARTY PARTY!

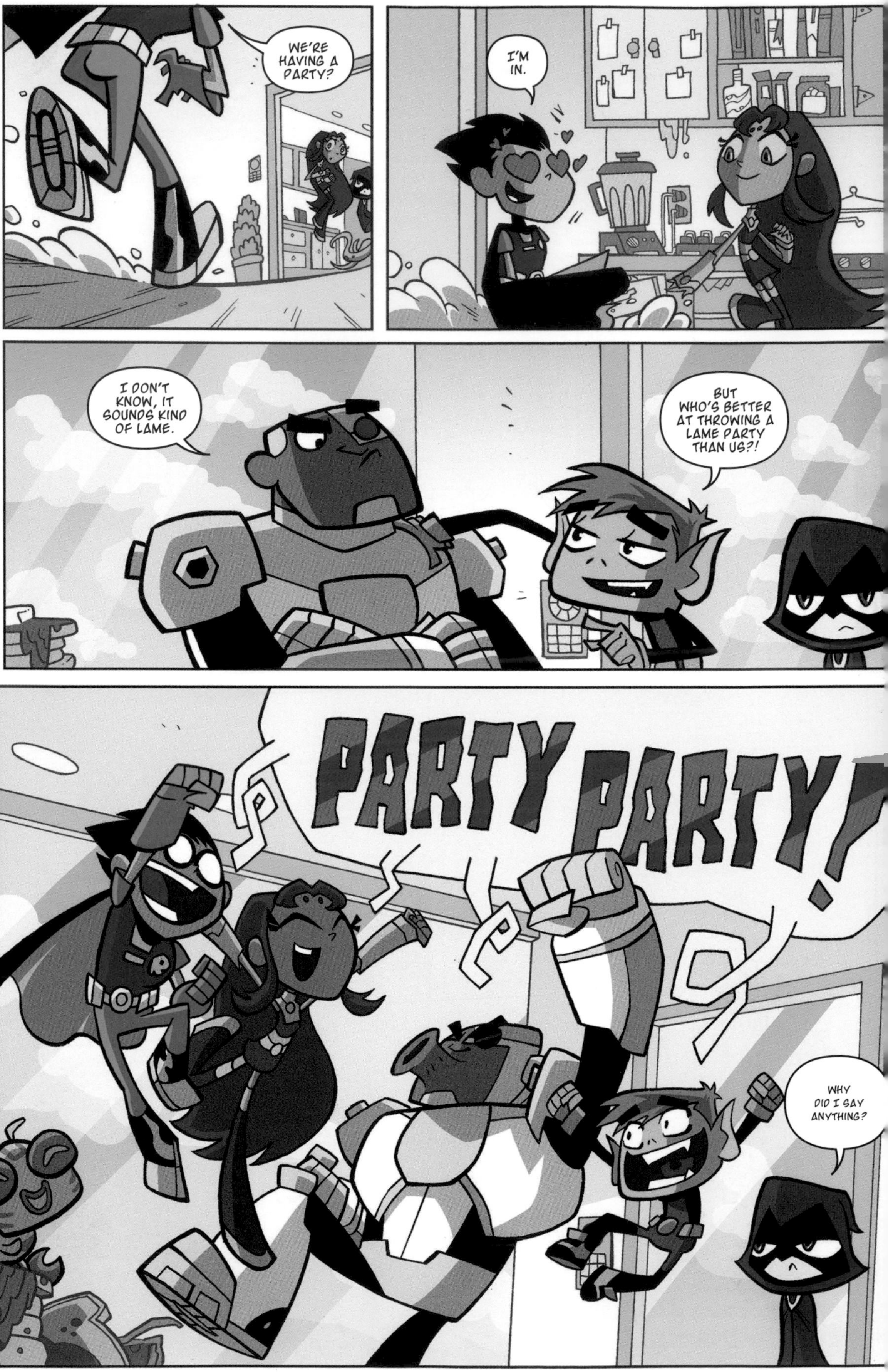
WE'RE HAVING A PARTY?
I'M IN.
I DON'T KNOW, IT SOUNDS KIND OF LAME.
BUT WHO'S BETTER AT THROWING A LAME PARTY THAN US?!
PARTY PARTY!
WHY DID I SAY ANYTHING?

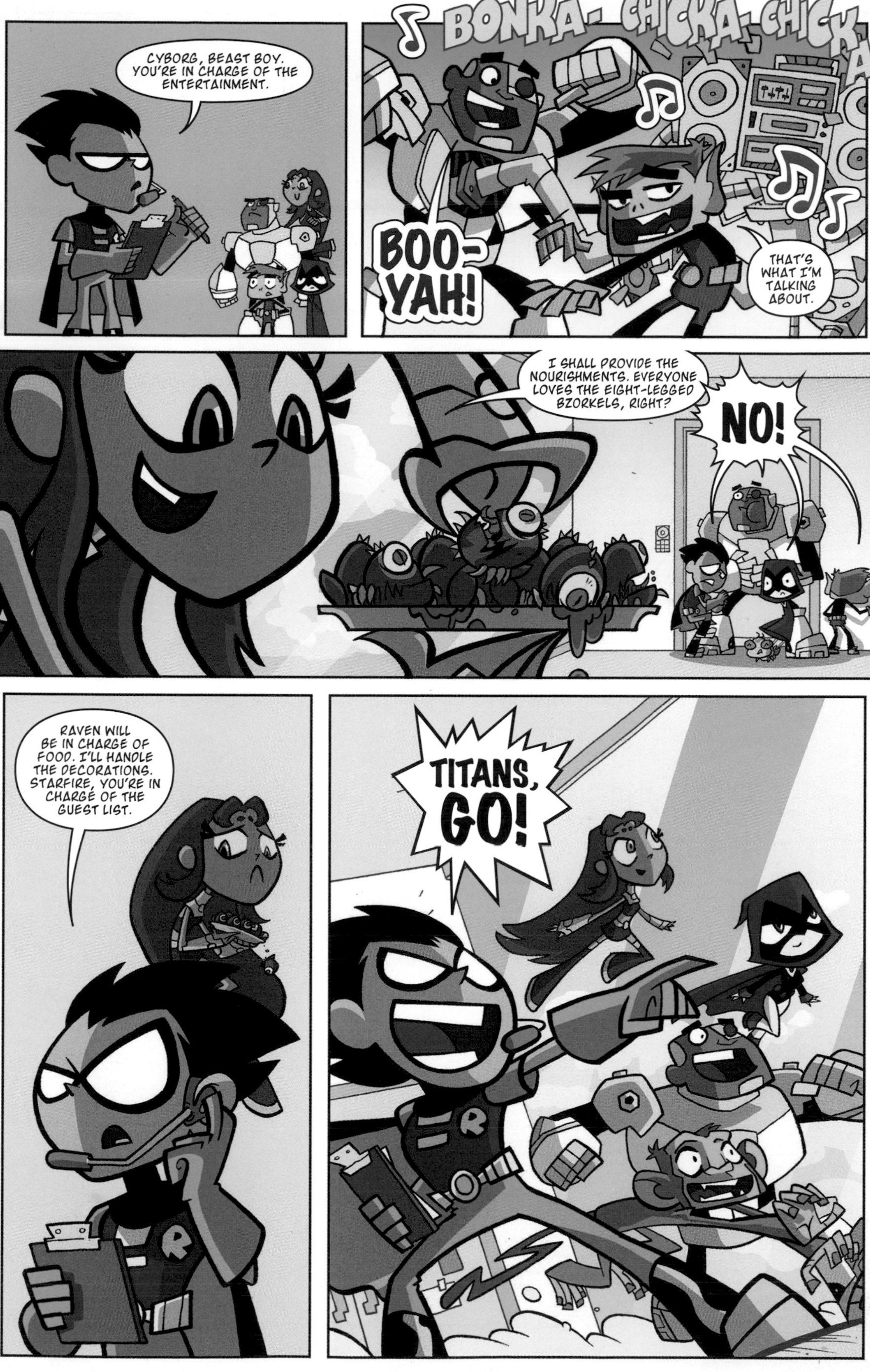
CYBORG, BEAST BOY. YOU'RE IN CHARGE OF THE ENTERTAINMENT.
BONKA-CHICKA-CHICKA
BOO-YAH!
THAT'S WHAT I'M TALKING ABOUT.
I SHALL PROVIDE THE NOURISHMENTS. EVERYONE LOVES THE EIGHT-LEGGED BZORKELS, RIGHT?
NO!
RAVEN WILL BE IN CHARGE OF FOOD. I'LL HANDLE THE DECORATIONS. STARFIRE, YOU'RE IN CHARGE OF THE GUEST LIST.
TITANS, GO!

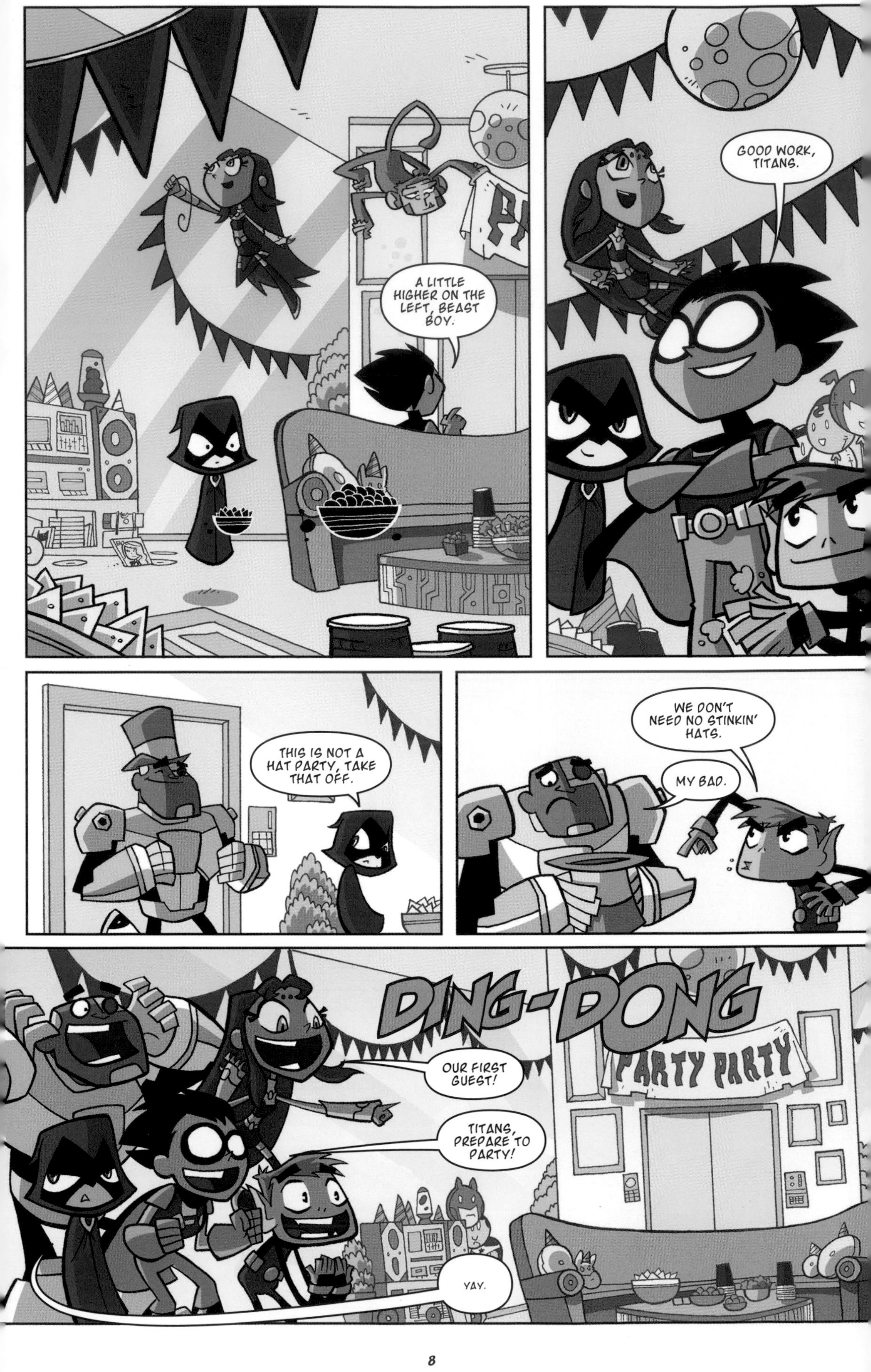
A LITTLE HIGHER ON THE LEFT, BEAST BOY.
GOOD WORK, TITANS.
THIS IS NOT A HAT PARTY, TAKE THAT OFF.
WE DON'T NEED NO STINKIN' HATS.
MY BAD.
DING-DONG
PARTY PARTY
OUR FIRST GUEST!
TITANS, PREPARE TO PARTY!
YAY.

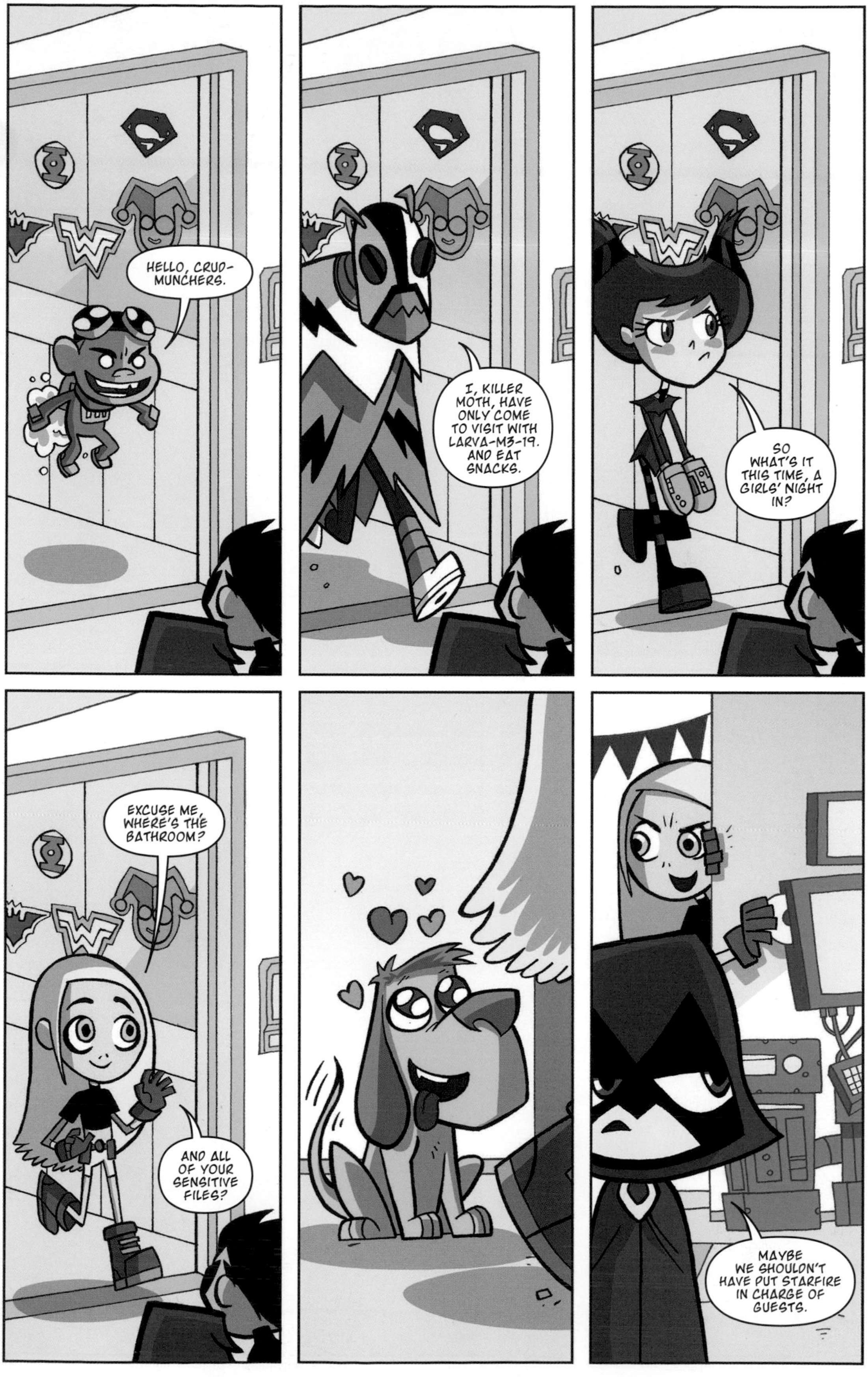
HELLO, CRUD-MUNCHERS.
I, KILLER MOTH, HAVE ONLY COME TO VISIT WITH LARVA-M3-19. AND EAT SNACKS.
SO WHAT'S IT THIS TIME, A GIRLS' NIGHT IN?
EXCUSE ME, WHERE'S THE BATHROOM?
AND ALL OF YOUR SENSITIVE FILES?
MAYBE WE SHOULDN'T HAVE PUT STARFIRE IN CHARGE OF GUESTS.

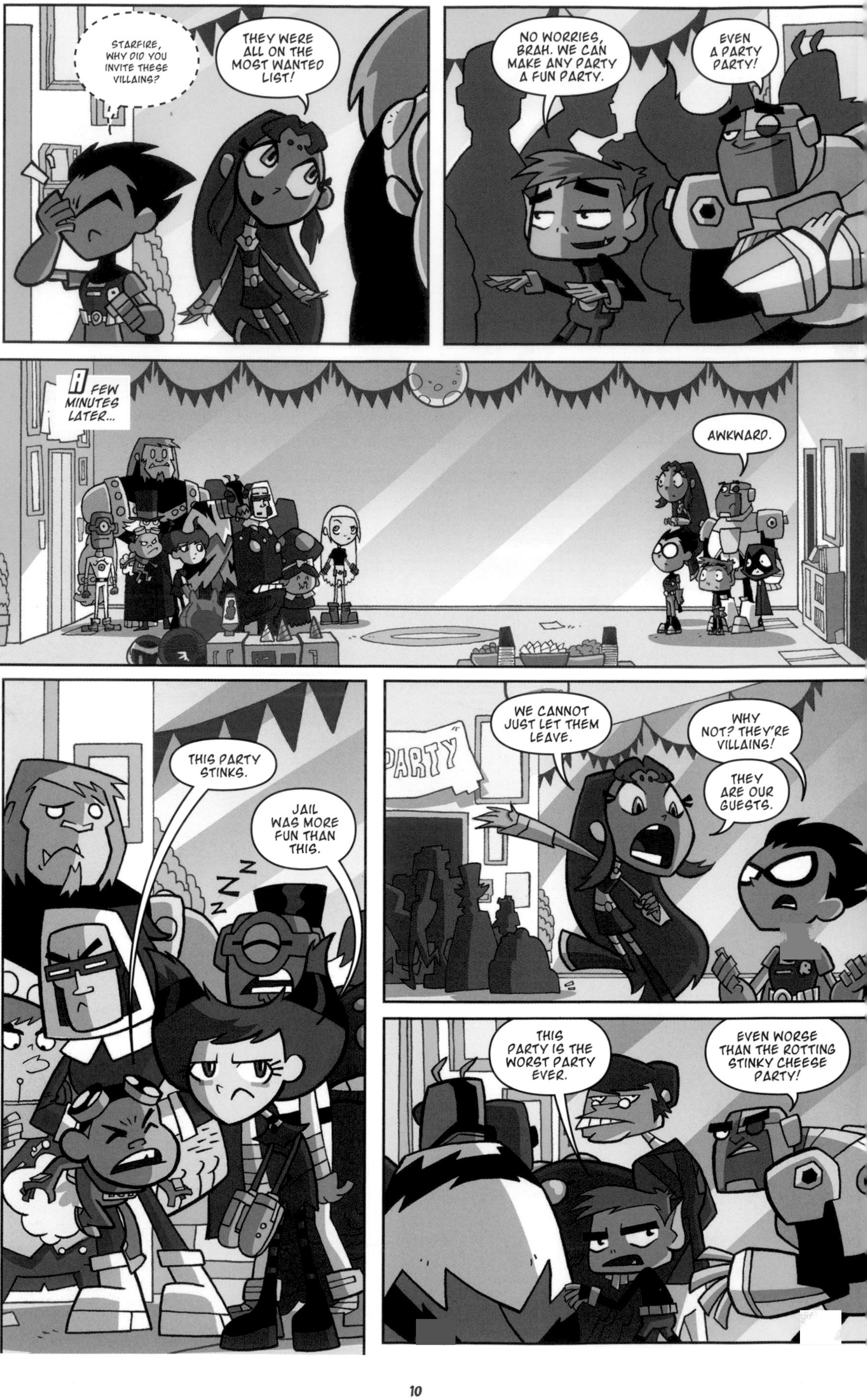
STARFIRE, WHY DID YOU INVITE THESE VILLAINS?
THEY WERE ALL ON THE MOST WANTED LIST!
NO WORRIES, BRAH. WE CAN MAKE ANY PARTY A FUN PARTY.
EVEN A PARTY PARTY!
A FEW MINUTES LATER...
AWKWARD.
THIS PARTY STINKS.
JAIL WAS MORE FUN THAN THIS.
ZZZ
PARTY
WE CANNOT JUST LET THEM LEAVE.
WHY NOT? THEY'RE VILLAINS!
THEY ARE OUR GUESTS.
THIS PARTY IS THE WORST PARTY EVER.
EVEN WORSE THAN THE ROTTING STINKY CHEESE PARTY!

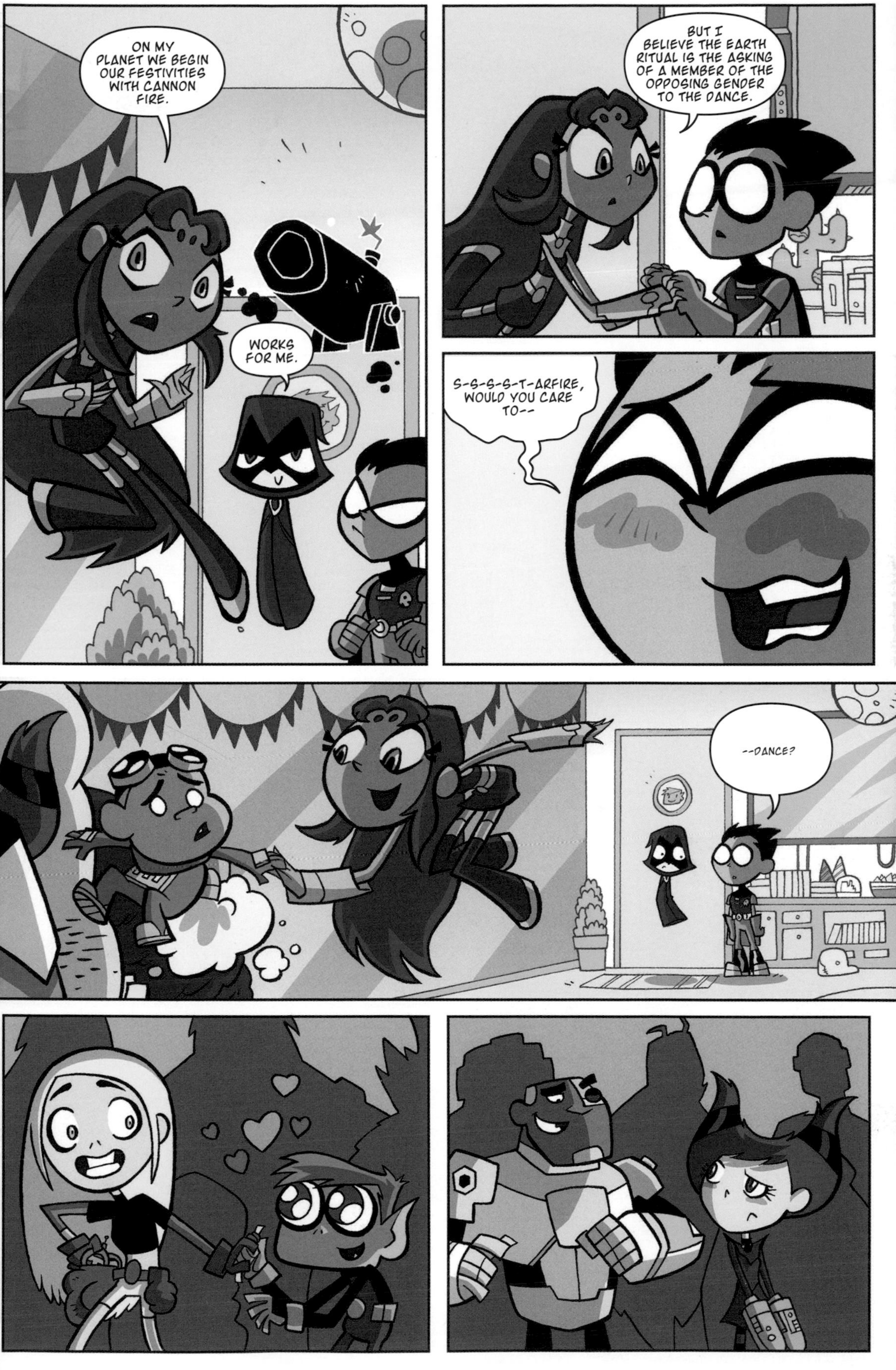
ON MY PLANET WE BEGIN OUR FESTIVITIES WITH CANNON FIRE.
WORKS FOR ME.
BUT I BELIEVE THE EARTH RITUAL IS THE ASKING OF A MEMBER OF THE OPPOSING GENDER TO THE DANCE.
S-S-S-S-T-ARFIRE, WOULD YOU CARE TO--
--DANCE?

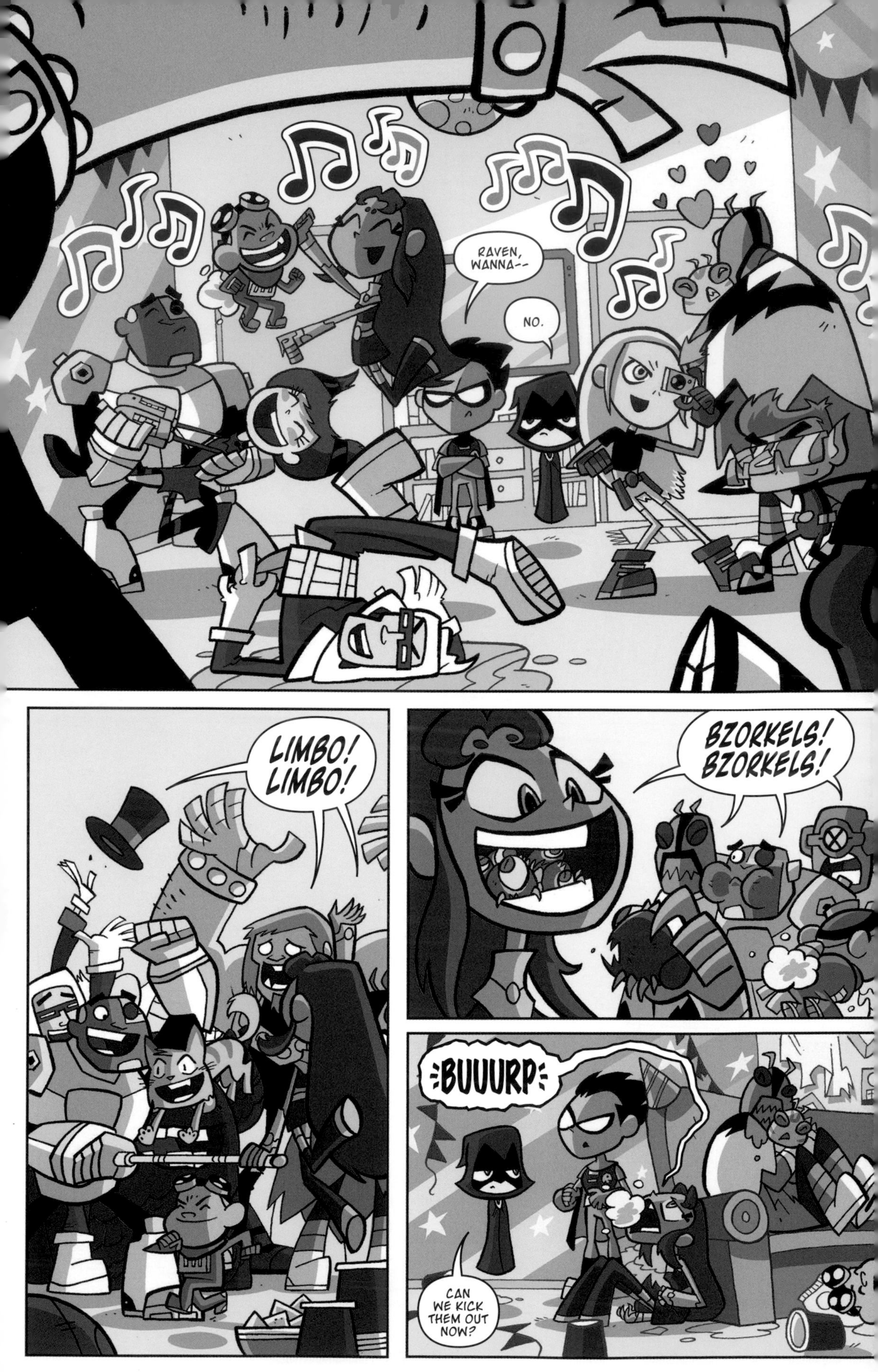

RAVEN, WANNA--
NO.
LIMBO! LIMBO!
BZORKELS! BZORKELS!
BUUURP
CAN WE KICK THEM OUT NOW?

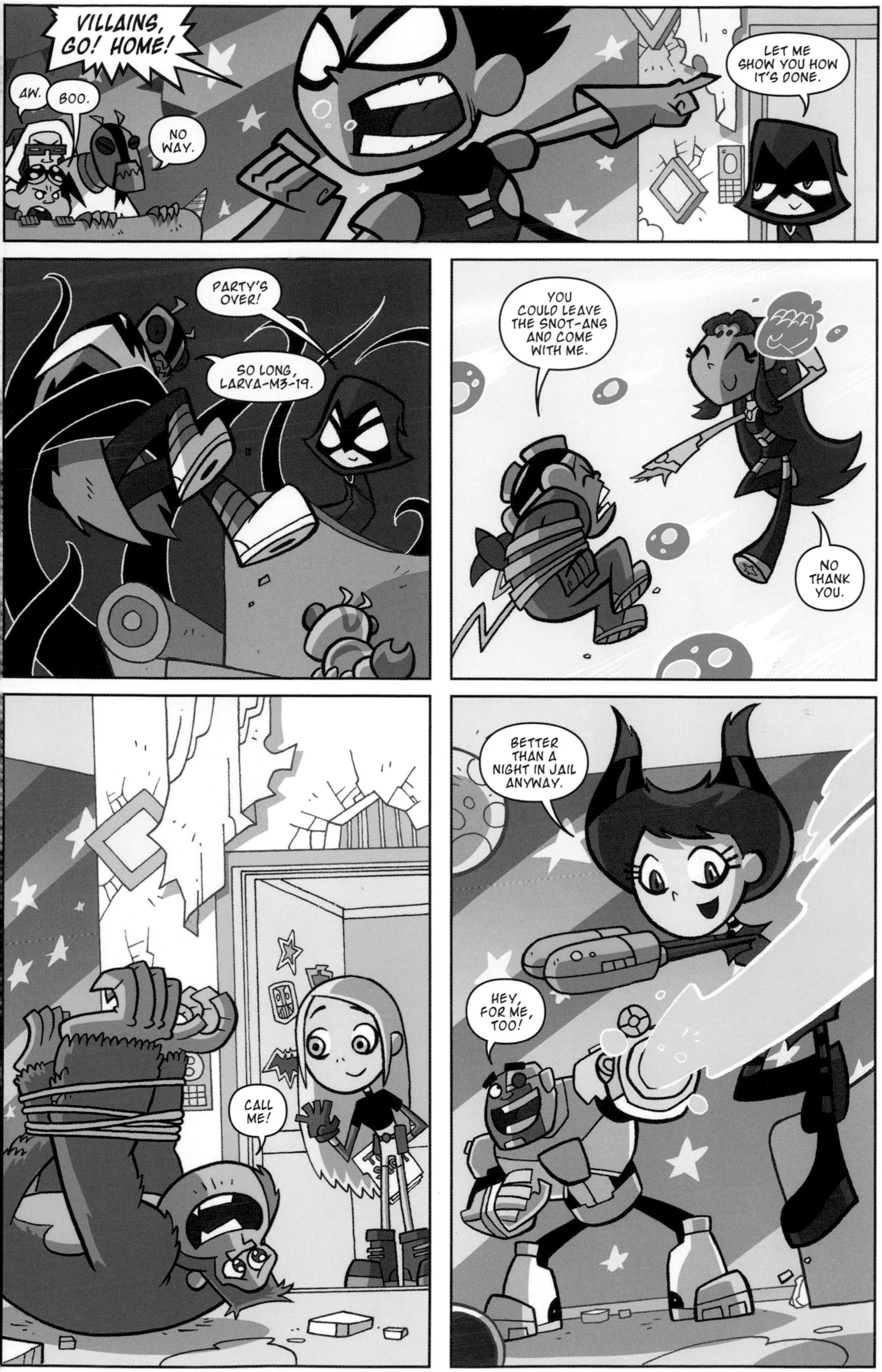
VILLAINS, GO! HOME!
AW.
BOO.
NO WAY.
LET ME SHOW YOU HOW IT'S DONE.
PARTY'S OVER!
SO LONG, LARVA-M3-19.
YOU COULD LEAVE THE SNOT-ANS AND COME WITH ME.
NO THANK YOU.
CALL ME!
BETTER THAN A NIGHT IN JAIL ANYWAY.
HEY, FOR ME, TOO!

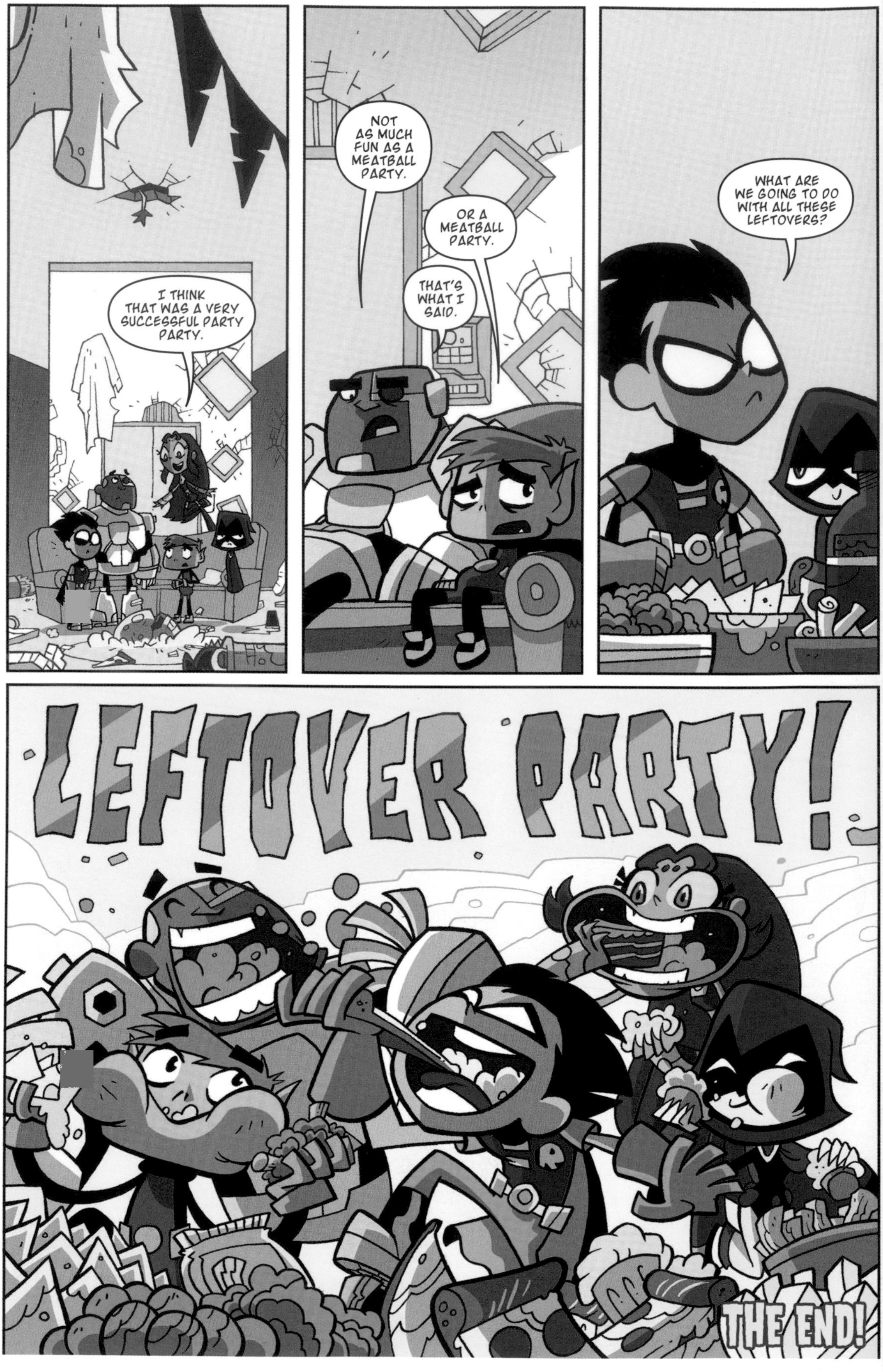
I THINK THAT WAS A VERY SUCCESSFUL PARTY PARTY.
NOT AS MUCH FUN AS A MEATBALL PARTY.
OR A MEATBALL PARTY.
THAT'S WHAT I SAID.
WHAT ARE WE GOING TO DO WITH ALL THESE LEFTOVERS?
LEFTOVER PARTY!
THE END!

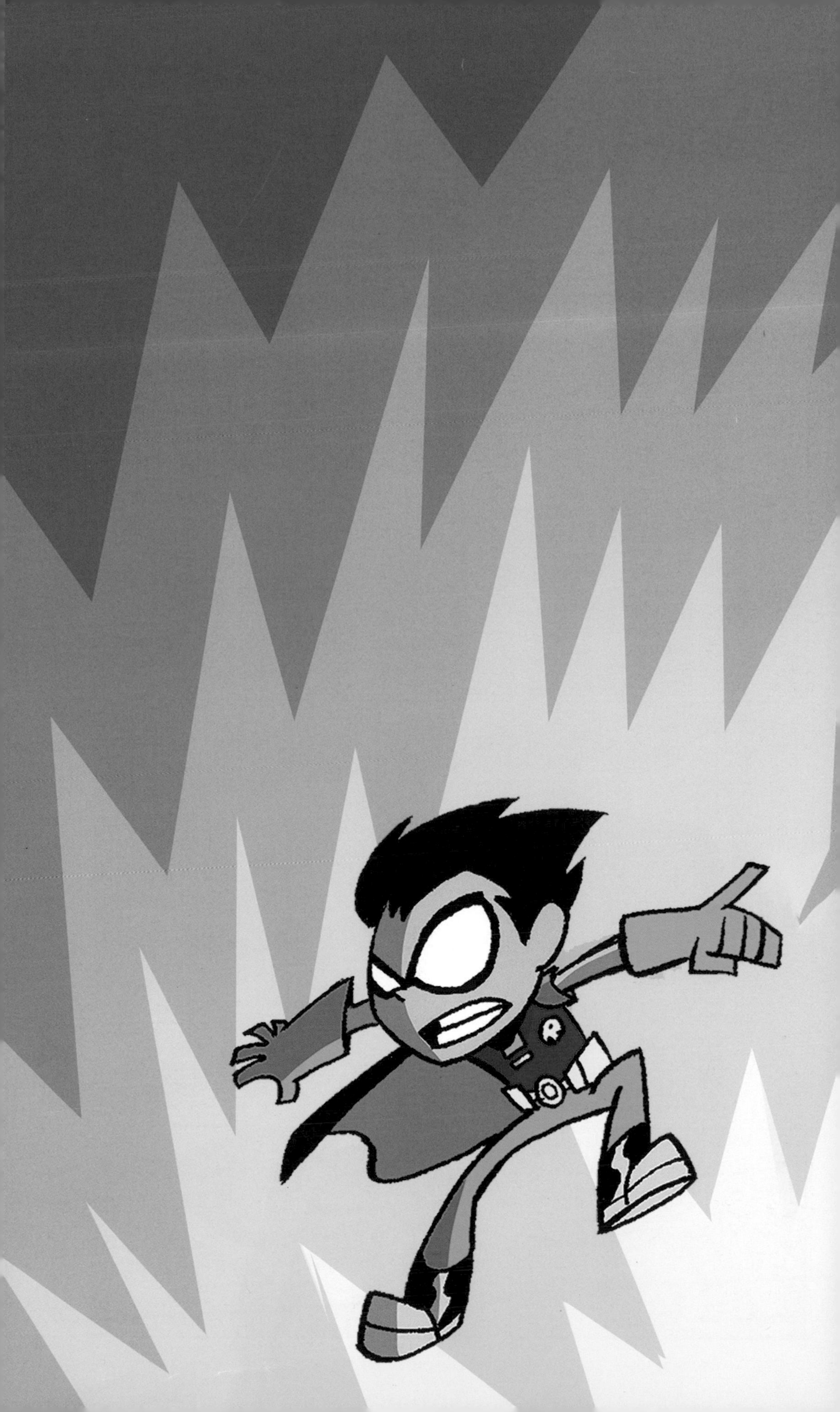

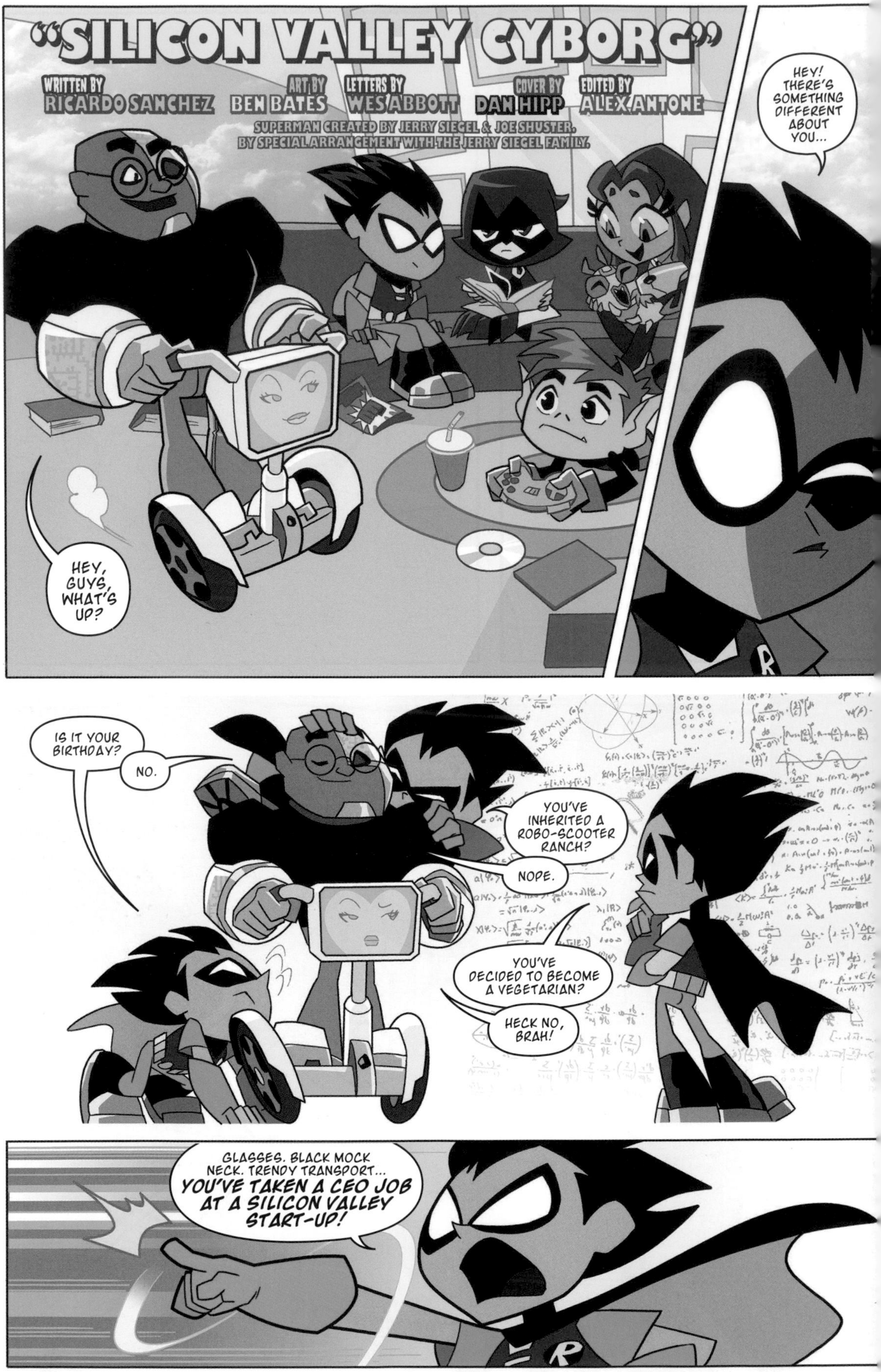
"SILICON VALLEY CYBORG"
WRITTEN BY RICARDO SANCHEZ
ART BY BEN BATES
LETTERS BY WES ABBOTT
COVER BY DAN HIPP
EDITED BY ALEX ANTONE
SUPERMAN CREATED BY JERRY SIEGEL & JOE SHUSTER.
BY SPECIAL ARRANGEMENT WITH THE JERRY SIEGEL FAMILY.
HEY, GUYS, WHAT'S UP?
HEY! THERE'S SOMETHING DIFFERENT ABOUT YOU...
IS IT YOUR BIRTHDAY?
NO.
YOU'VE INHERITED A ROBO-SCOOTER RANCH?
NOPE.
YOU'VE DECIDED TO BECOME A VEGETARIAN?
HECK NO, BRAH!
GLASSES. BLACK MOCK NECK. TRENDY TRANSPORT... YOU'VE TAKEN A CEO JOB AT A SILICON VALLEY START-UP!

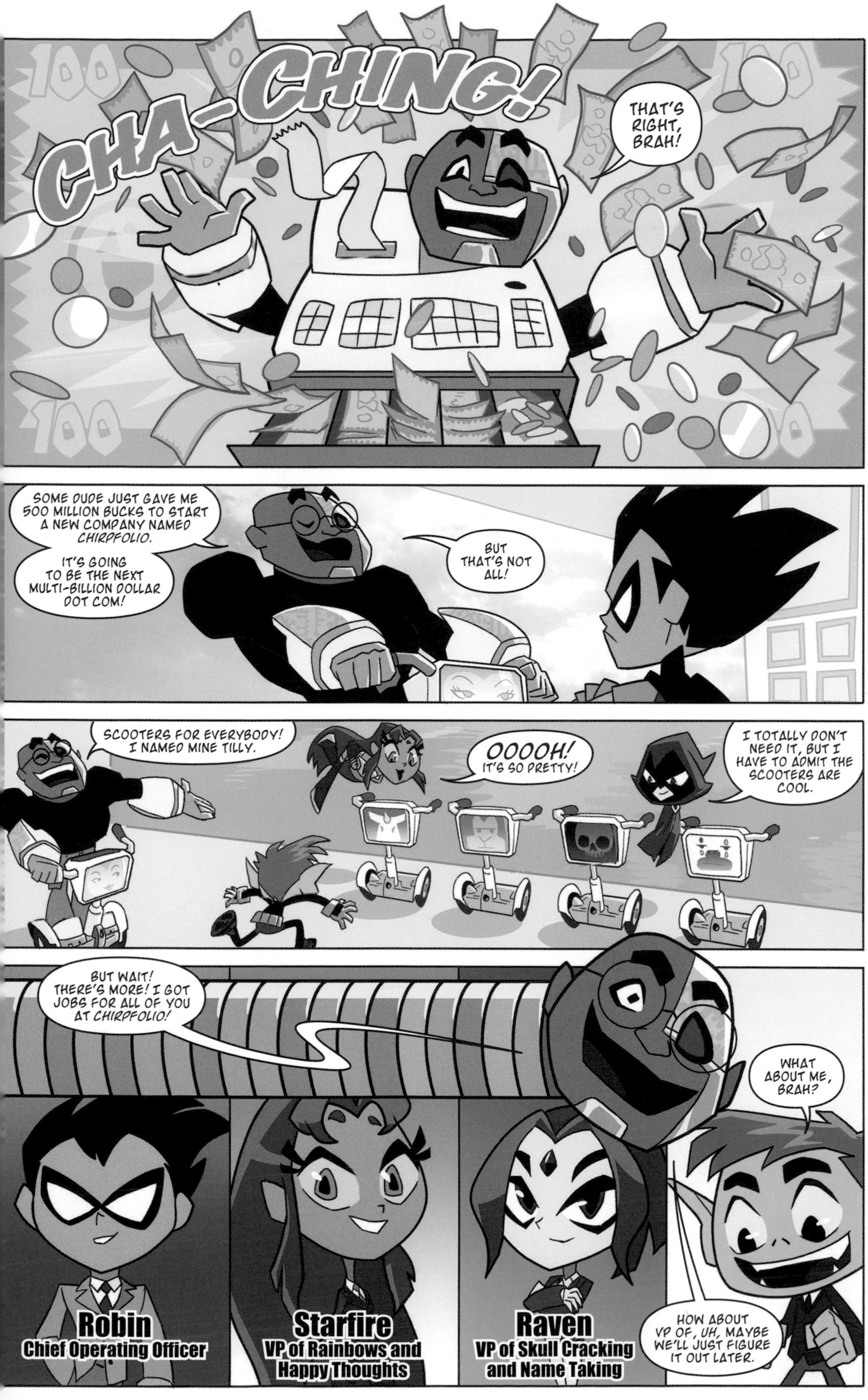
CHA-CHING!
THAT'S RIGHT, BRAH!
SOME DUDE JUST GAVE ME 500 MILLION BUCKS TO START A NEW COMPANY NAMED CHIRPFOLIO.
IT'S GOING TO BE THE NEXT MULTI-BILLION DOLLAR DOT COM!
BUT THAT'S NOT ALL!
SCOOTERS FOR EVERYBODY! I NAMED MINE TILLY.
OOOOH! IT'S SO PRETTY!
I TOTALLY DON'T NEED IT, BUT I HAVE TO ADMIT THE SCOOTERS ARE COOL.
BUT WAIT! THERE'S MORE! I GOT JOBS FOR ALL OF YOU AT CHIRPFOLIO!
WHAT ABOUT ME, BRAH?
Robin
Chief Operating Officer
Starfire
VP of Rainbows and Happy Thoughts
Raven
VP of Skull Cracking and Name Taking
HOW ABOUT VP OF, UH, MAYBE WE'LL JUST FIGURE IT OUT LATER.

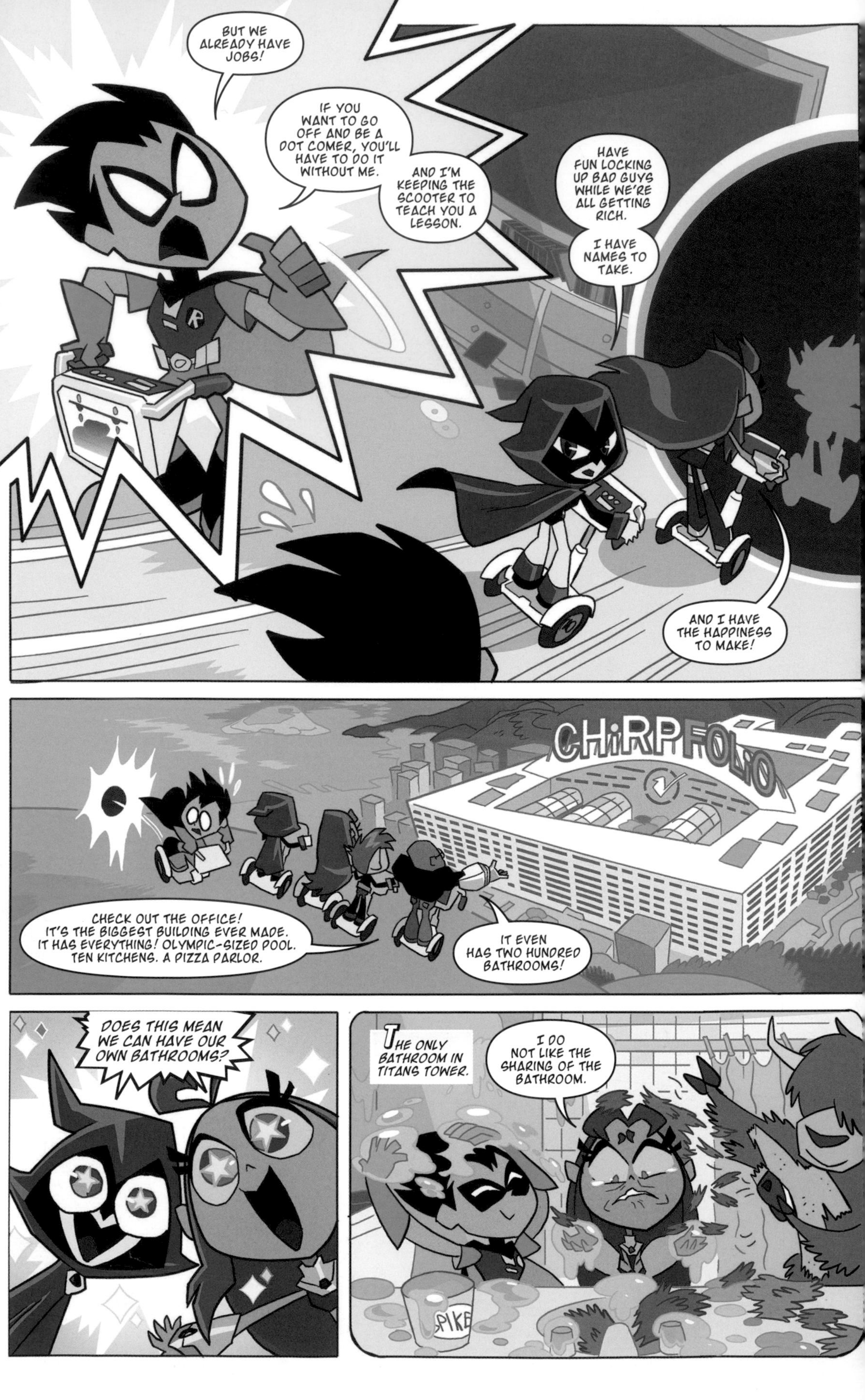
BUT WE ALREADY HAVE JOBS!
IF YOU WANT TO GO OFF AND BE A DOT COMER, YOU'LL HAVE TO DO IT WITHOUT ME.
AND I'M KEEPING THE SCOOTER TO TEACH YOU A LESSON.
HAVE FUN LOCKING UP BAD GUYS WHILE WE'RE ALL GETTING RICH.
I HAVE NAMES TO TAKE.
AND I HAVE THE HAPPINESS TO MAKE!
CHiRPFOLiO
CHECK OUT THE OFFICE! IT'S THE BIGGEST BUILDING EVER MADE. IT HAS EVERYTHING! OLYMPIC-SIZED POOL. TEN KITCHENS. A PIZZA PARLOR.
IT EVEN HAS TWO HUNDRED BATHROOMS!
DOES THIS MEAN WE CAN HAVE OUR OWN BATHROOMS?
THE ONLY BATHROOM IN TITANS TOWER.
I DO NOT LIKE THE SHARING OF THE BATHROOM.
SPIKE

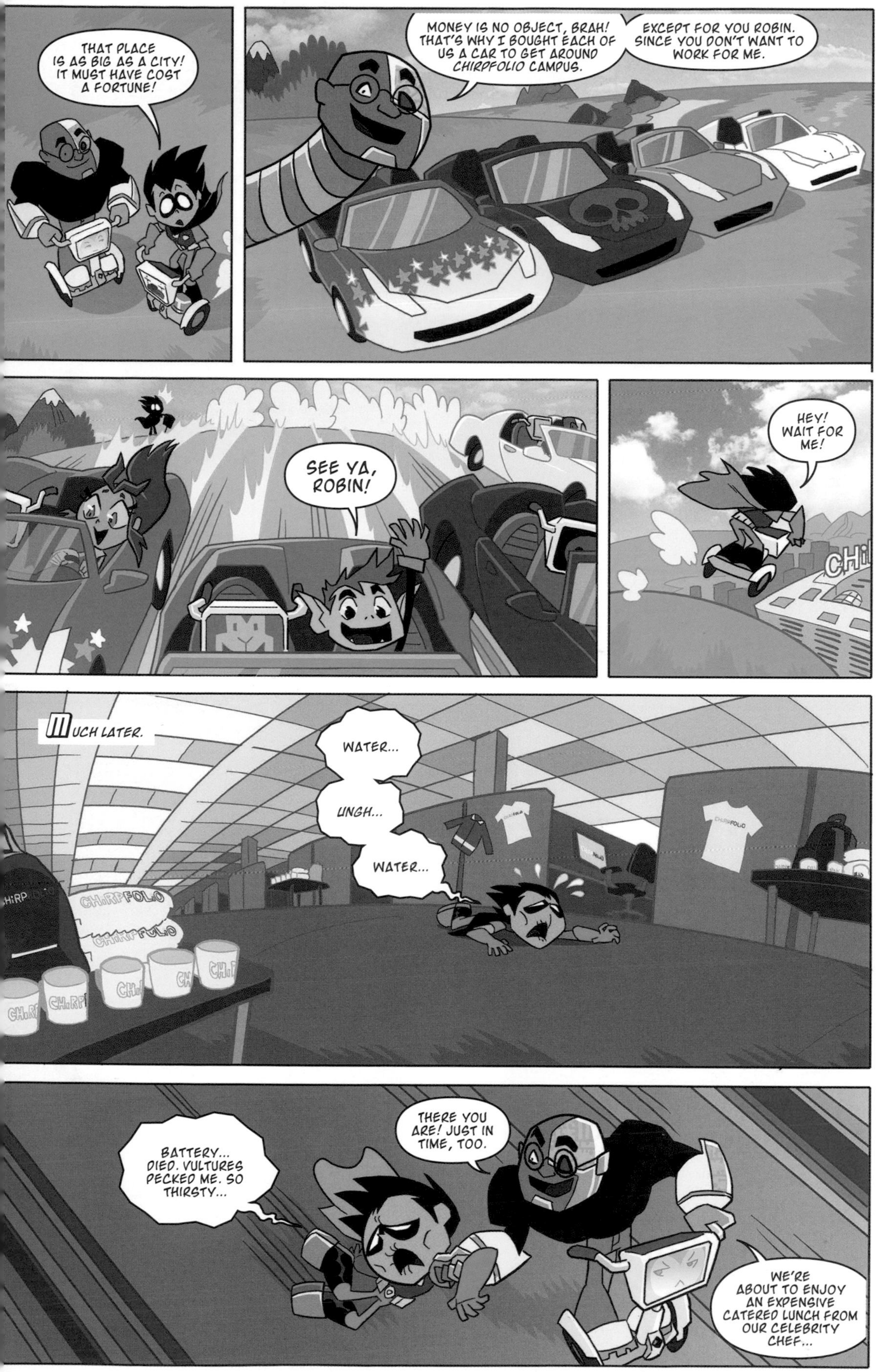
THAT PLACE IS AS BIG AS A CITY! IT MUST HAVE COST A FORTUNE!
MONEY IS NO OBJECT, BRAH! THAT'S WHY I BOUGHT EACH OF US A CAR TO GET AROUND CHIRPFOLIO CAMPUS.
EXCEPT FOR YOU ROBIN. SINCE YOU DON'T WANT TO WORK FOR ME.
SEE YA, ROBIN!
HEY! WAIT FOR ME!
MUCH LATER.
WATER...
UNGH...
WATER...
CHIRPFOLIO
THERE YOU ARE! JUST IN TIME, TOO.
BATTERY... DIED. VULTURES PECKED ME. SO THIRSTY...
WE'RE ABOUT TO ENJOY AN EXPENSIVE CATERED LUNCH FROM OUR CELEBRITY CHEF...

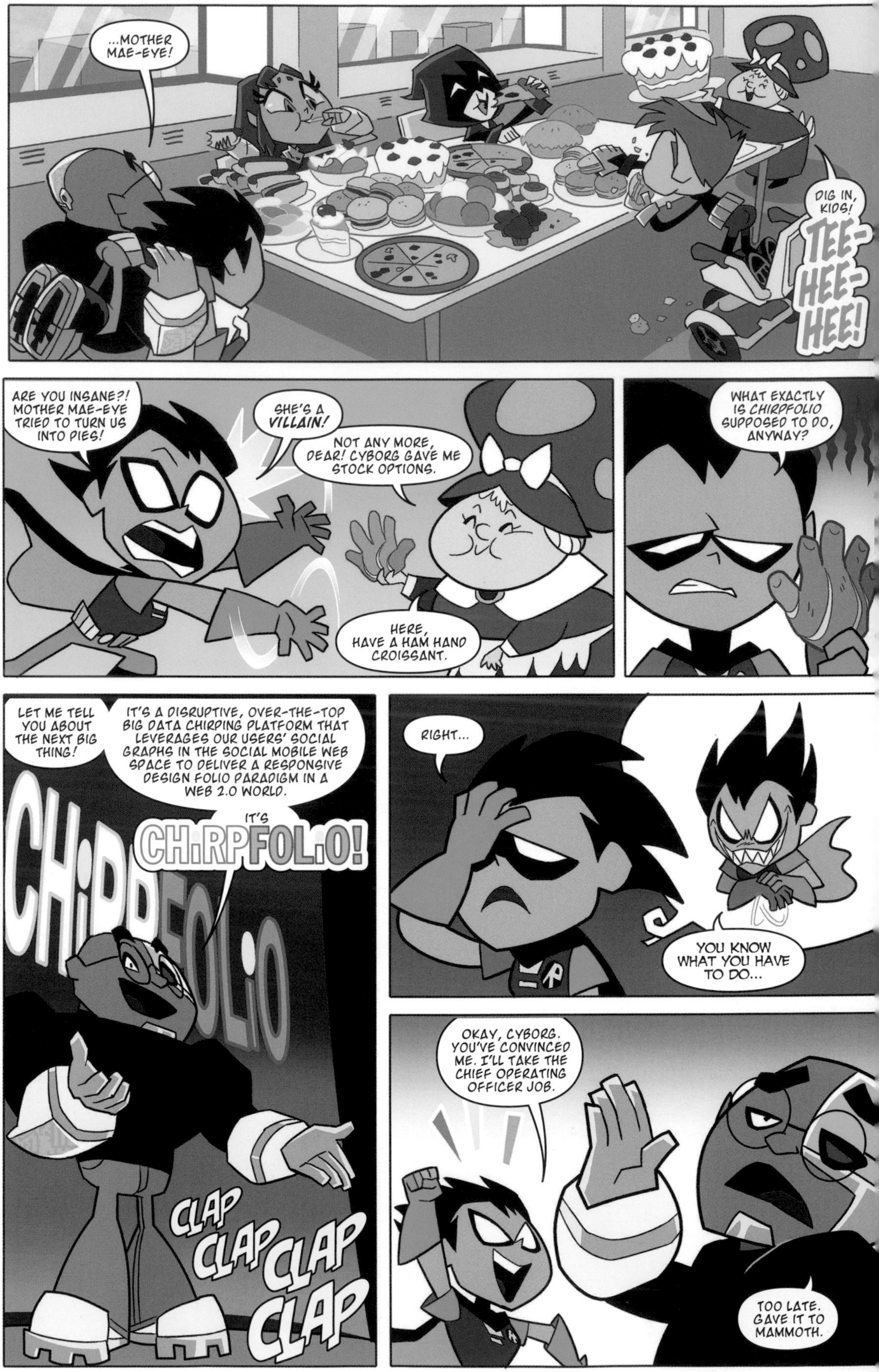

...MOTHER MAE-EYE!
DIG IN, KIDS!
TEE-HEE-HEE!
ARE YOU INSANE?! MOTHER MAE-EYE TRIED TO TURN US INTO PIES!
SHE'S A VILLAIN!
NOT ANY MORE, DEAR! CYBORG GAVE ME STOCK OPTIONS.
HERE, HAVE A HAM HAND CROISSANT.
WHAT EXACTLY IS CHIRPFOLIO SUPPOSED TO DO, ANYWAY?
LET ME TELL YOU ABOUT THE NEXT BIG THING!
IT'S A DISRUPTIVE, OVER-THE-TOP BIG DATA CHIRPING PLATFORM THAT LEVERAGES OUR USERS' SOCIAL GRAPHS IN THE SOCIAL MOBILE WEB SPACE TO DELIVER A RESPONSIVE DESIGN FOLIO PARADIGM IN A WEB 2.0 WORLD.
IT'S CHIRPFOLIO!
CLAP CLAP CLAP CLAP
RIGHT...
YOU KNOW WHAT YOU HAVE TO DO...
OKAY, CYBORG. YOU'VE CONVINCED ME. I'LL TAKE THE CHIEF OPERATING OFFICER JOB.
TOO LATE. GAVE IT TO MAMMOTH.

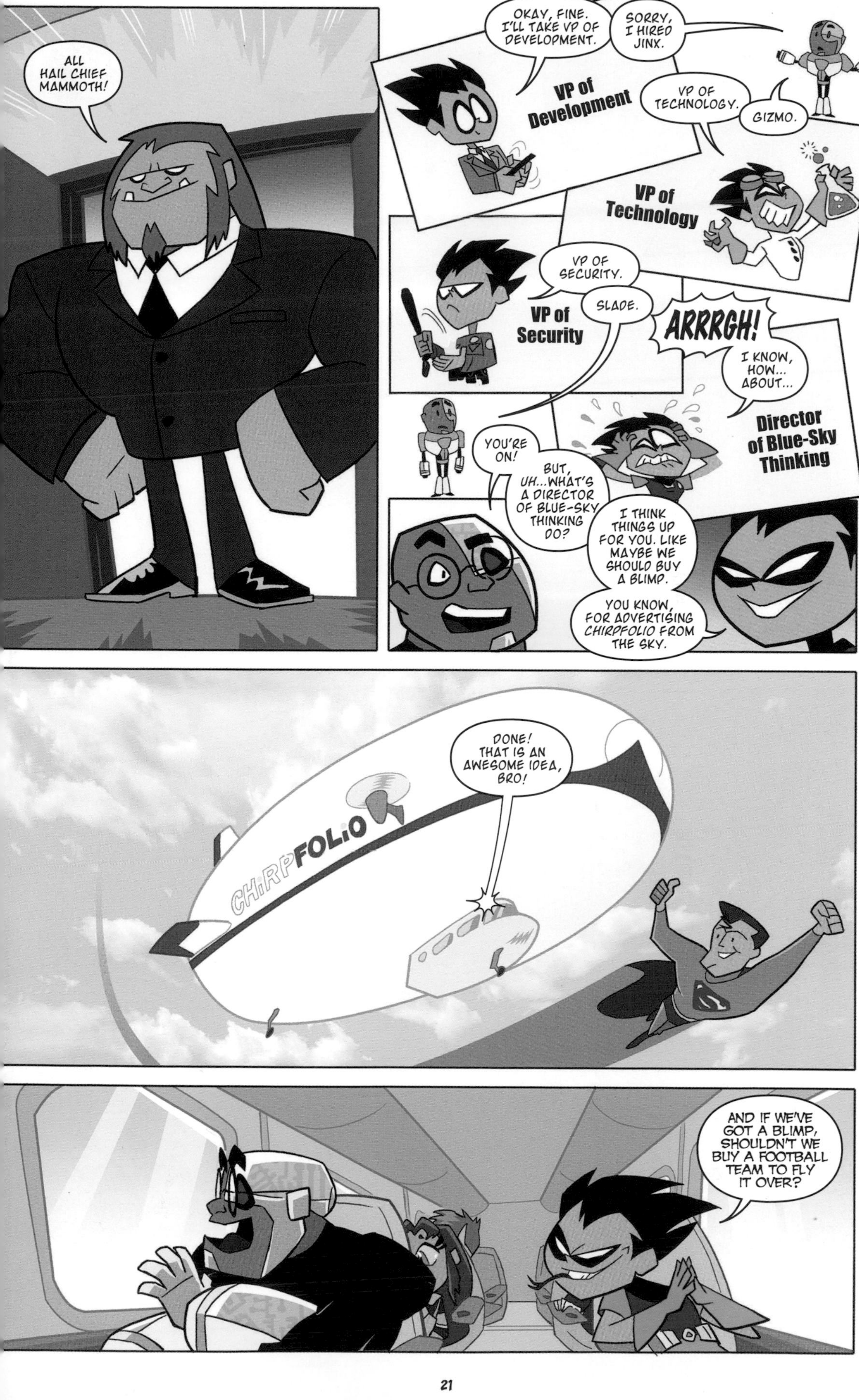

ALL HAIL CHIEF MAMMOTH!
OKAY, FINE. I'LL TAKE VP OF DEVELOPMENT.
SORRY, I HIRED JINX.
VP of Development
VP OF TECHNOLOGY.
GIZMO.
VP of Technology
VP OF SECURITY.
SLADE.
VP of Security
ARRRGH!
I KNOW, HOW... ABOUT...
Director of Blue-Sky Thinking
YOU'RE ON!
BUT, UH...WHAT'S A DIRECTOR OF BLUE-SKY THINKING DO?
I THINK THINGS UP FOR YOU. LIKE MAYBE WE SHOULD BUY A BLIMP.
YOU KNOW, FOR ADVERTISING CHIRPFOLIO FROM THE SKY.
DONE! THAT IS AN AWESOME IDEA, BRO!
CHIRPFOLIO
AND IF WE'VE GOT A BLIMP, SHOULDN'T WE BUY A FOOTBALL TEAM TO FLY IT OVER?

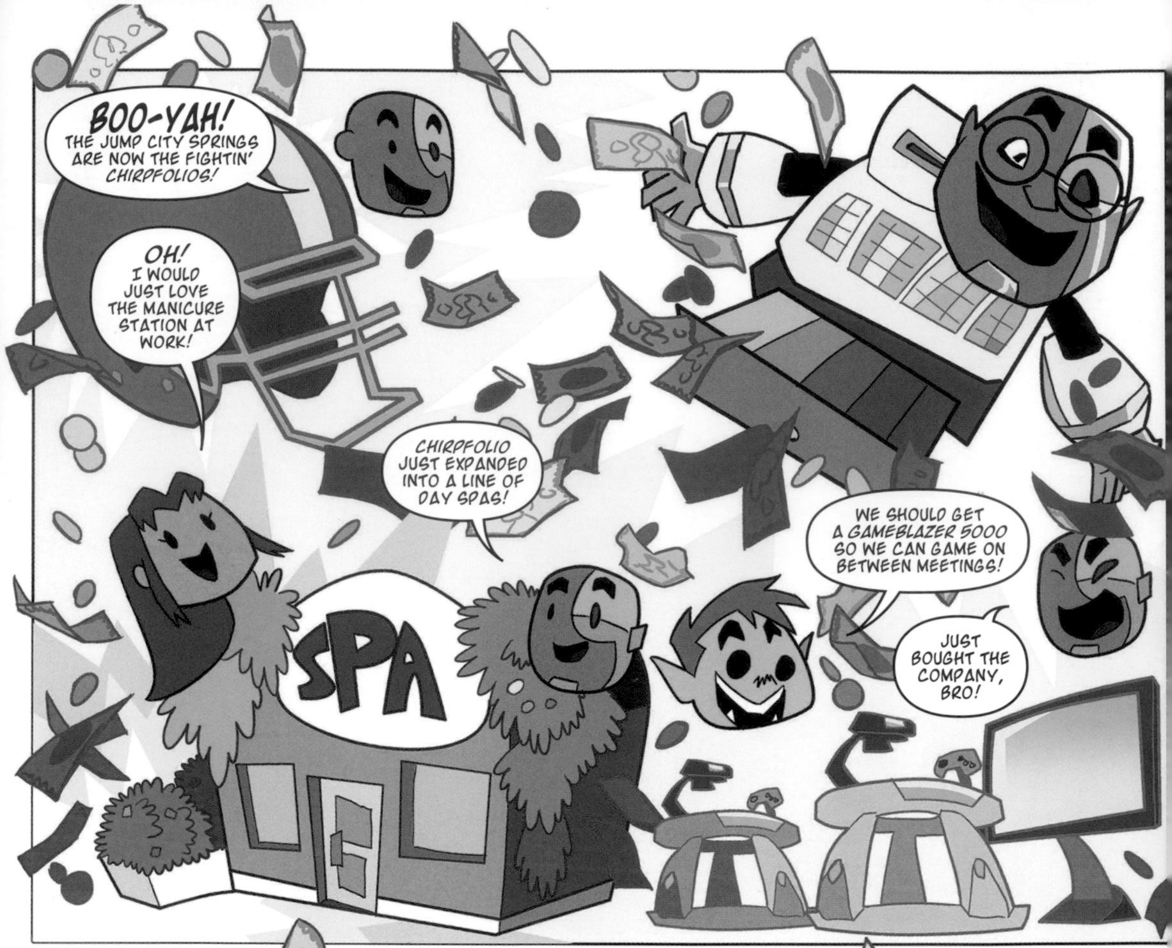
BOO-YAH! THE JUMP CITY SPRINGS ARE NOW THE FIGHTIN' CHIRPFOLIOS!
OH! I WOULD JUST LOVE THE MANICURE STATION AT WORK!
CHIRPFOLIO JUST EXPANDED INTO A LINE OF DAY SPAS!
SPA
WE SHOULD GET A GAMEBLAZER 5000 SO WE CAN GAME ON BETWEEN MEETINGS!
JUST BOUGHT THE COMPANY, BRO!

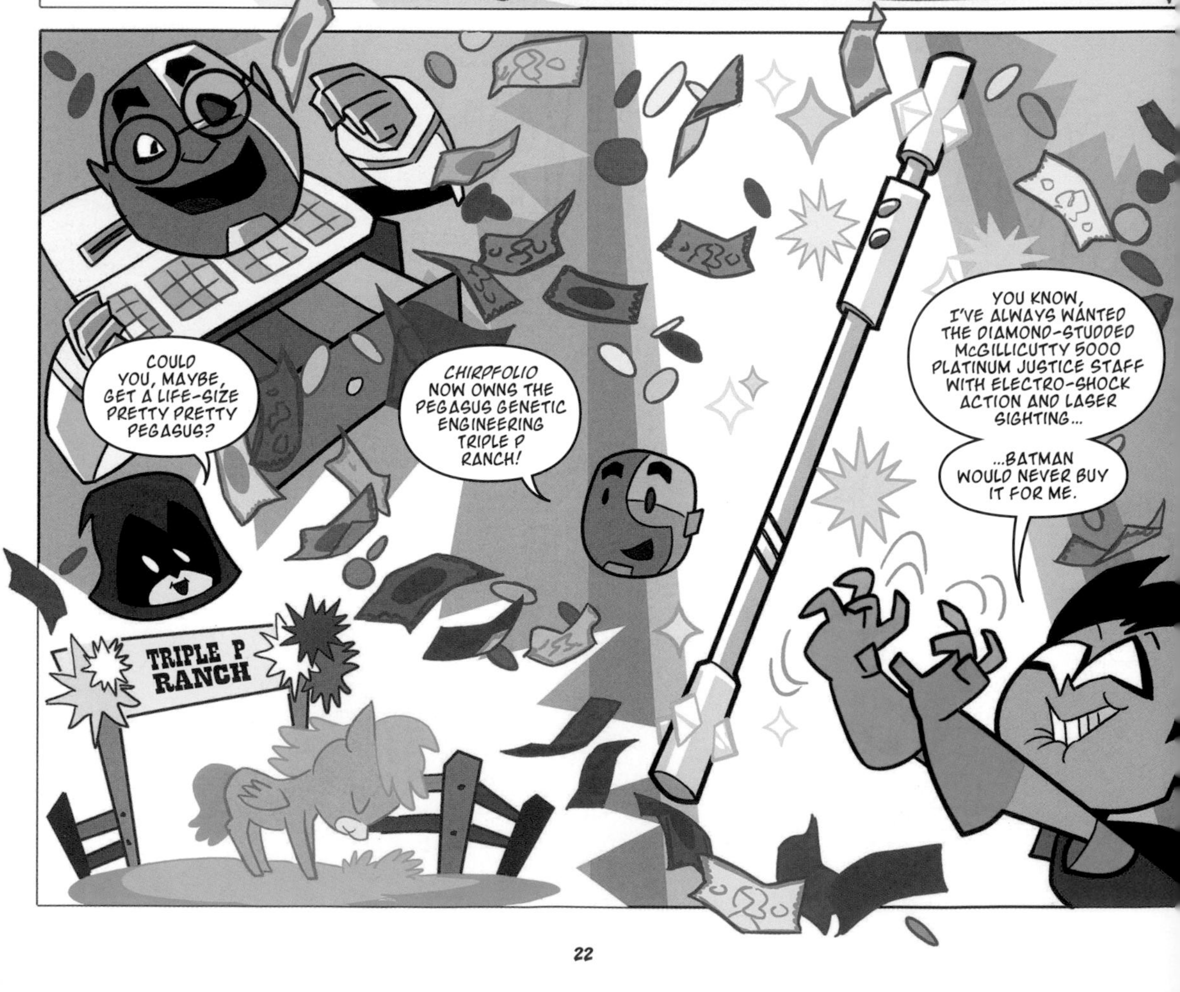
COULD YOU, MAYBE, GET A LIFE-SIZE PRETTY PRETTY PEGASUS?
CHIRPFOLIO NOW OWNS THE PEGASUS GENETIC ENGINEERING TRIPLE P RANCH!
TRIPLE P RANCH
YOU KNOW, I'VE ALWAYS WANTED THE DIAMOND-STUDDED McGILLICUTTY 5000 PLATINUM JUSTICE STAFF WITH ELECTRO-SHOCK ACTION AND LASER SIGHTING...
...BATMAN WOULD NEVER BUY IT FOR ME.

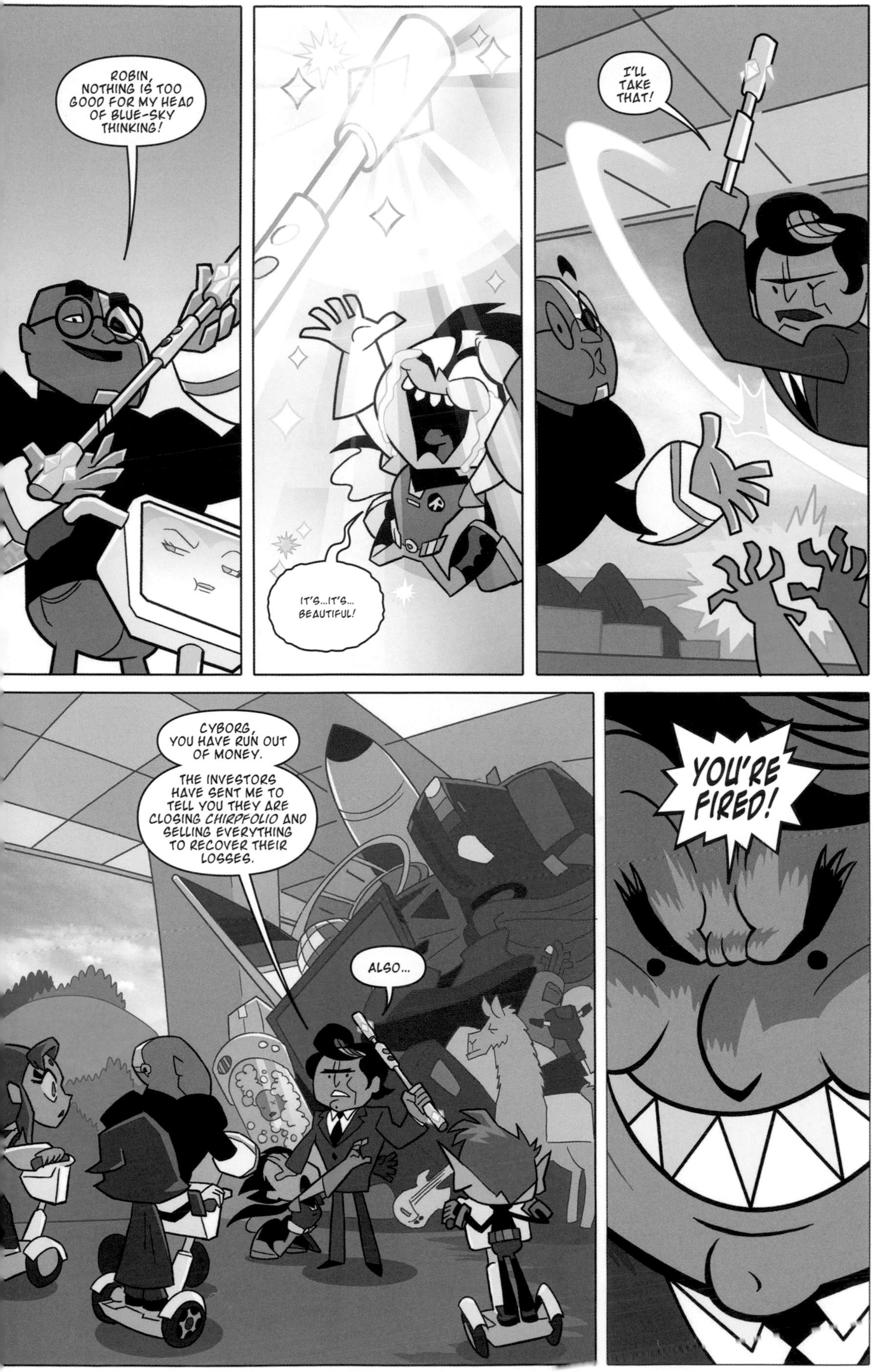
ROBIN, NOTHING IS TOO GOOD FOR MY HEAD OF BLUE-SKY THINKING!
IT'S...IT'S... BEAUTIFUL!
I'LL TAKE THAT!
CYBORG, YOU HAVE RUN OUT OF MONEY.
THE INVESTORS HAVE SENT ME TO TELL YOU THEY ARE CLOSING CHIRPFOLIO AND SELLING EVERYTHING TO RECOVER THEIR LOSSES.
ALSO...
YOU'RE FIRED!

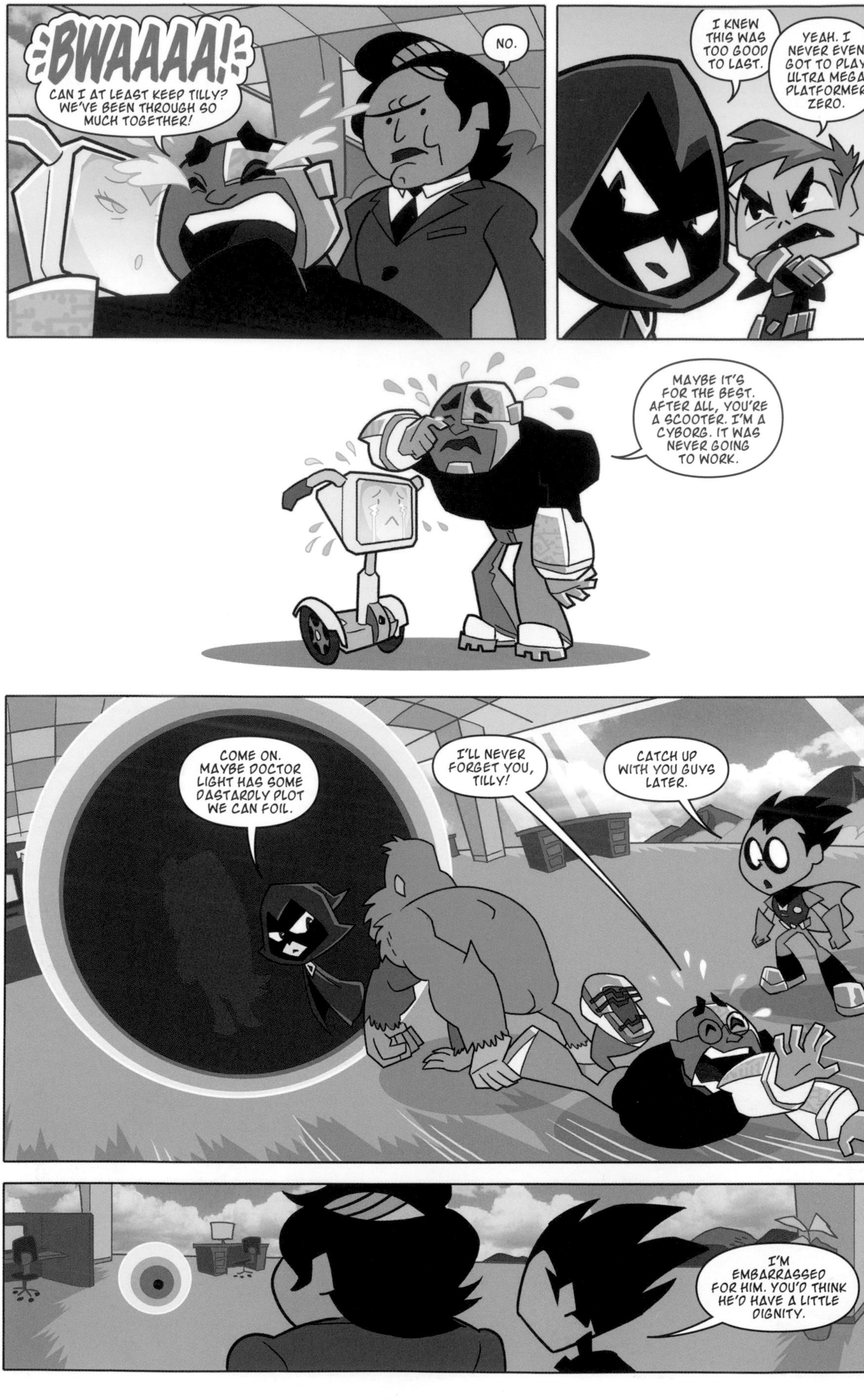
BWAAAA!
CAN I AT LEAST KEEP TILLY? WE'VE BEEN THROUGH SO MUCH TOGETHER!
NO.
I KNEW THIS WAS TOO GOOD TO LAST.
YEAH. I NEVER EVEN GOT TO PLAY ULTRA MEGA PLATFORMER ZERO.
MAYBE IT'S FOR THE BEST. AFTER ALL, YOU'RE A SCOOTER. I'M A CYBORG. IT WAS NEVER GOING TO WORK.
COME ON. MAYBE DOCTOR LIGHT HAS SOME DASTARDLY PLOT WE CAN FOIL.
I'LL NEVER FORGET YOU, TILLY!
CATCH UP WITH YOU GUYS LATER.
I'M EMBARRASSED FOR HIM. YOU'D THINK HE'D HAVE A LITTLE DIGNITY.

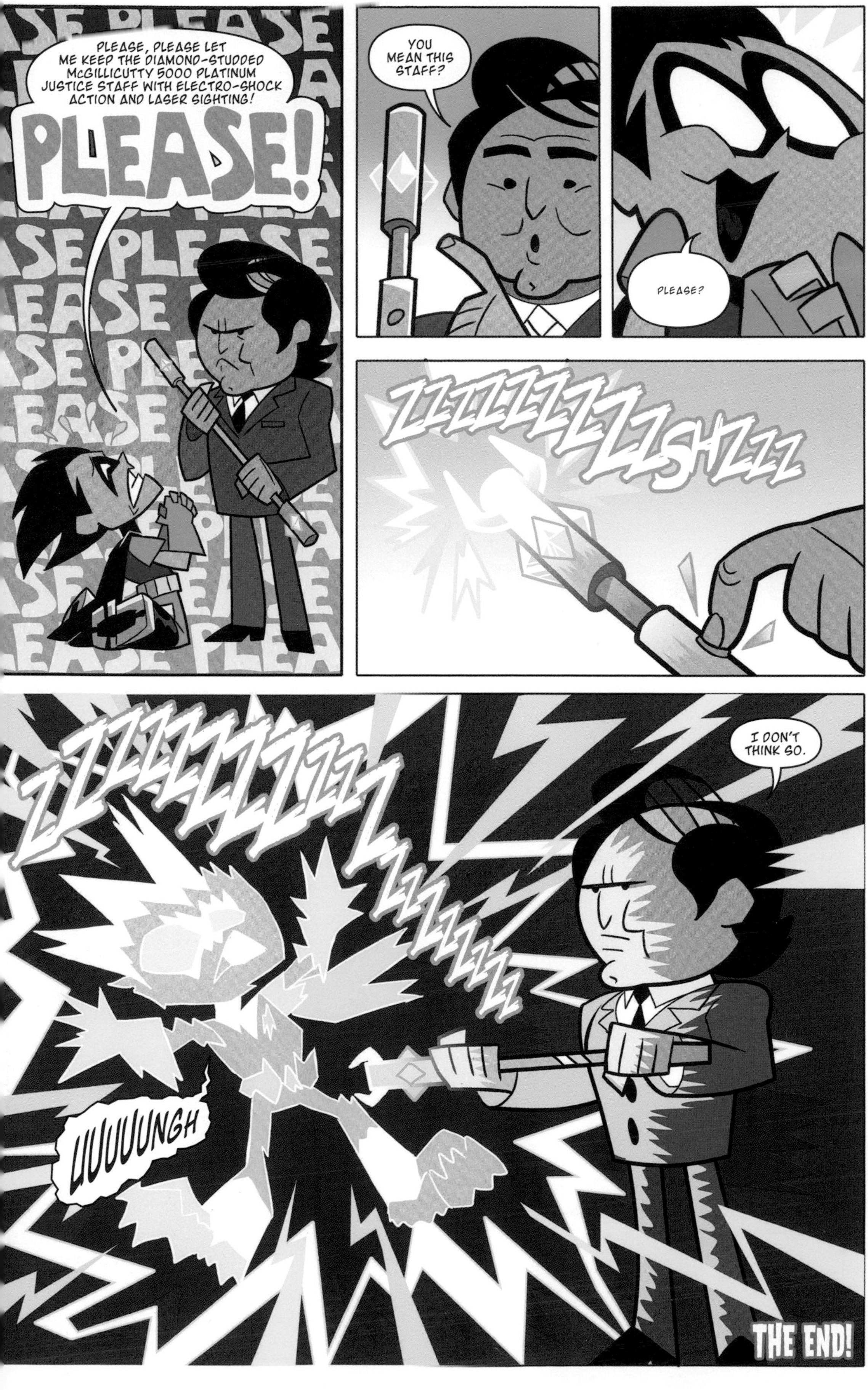
PLEASE, PLEASE LET ME KEEP THE DIAMOND-STUDDED McGILLICUTTY 5000 PLATINUM JUSTICE STAFF WITH ELECTRO-SHOCK ACTION AND LASER SIGHTING!
PLEASE!
YOU MEAN THIS STAFF?
PLEASE?
ZZZZZZZZZZZSHZZZ
I DON'T THINK SO.
UUUUUNGH
THE END!

CREATORS

AMY WOLFRAM

Amy Wolfram is a comic book and television writer. She has written episodes for the animated TV series *Teen Titans*, *Legion of Super-Heroes*, and *Teen Titans Go!*. In addition to the *Teen Titans Go!* comic book series, she has also written for *Teen Titans: Year One*.

RICARDO SANCHEZ

Ricardo Sanchez is a writer, Emmy winning creator, and executive producer. His comic book credits include *Batman: Legends of the Dark Knight*, *Resident Evil*, *RIFT: Telara Chronicles*, and many others. When he's not writing comics, Ricardo maintains a vintage toy blog, drives 70's muscle cars, and shops year round for Halloween decorations for his home in Redwood City, California.

JORGE CORONA

Jorge Corona is a Venezuelan comic artist who is well-known for his all-ages fantasy-adventure series *Feathers* and his work on *Jim Henson's The Storyteller: Dragons*. In addition to *Teen Titans Go!*, he has also worked on *Batman Beyond*, *Justice League Beyond*, *We Are Robin*, *Goners*, and many other comics.

BEN BATES

Ben Bates is a comic book illustrator, colorist, and writer. In addition to *Teen Titans Go!*, he has also worked on *Teenage Mutant Ninja Turtles*, *Mega Man*, *My Little Pony*, and many other comics.

GLOSSARY

advertising (AD-vuhr-tyz-ing)—using words and pictures to encourage people to buy a product

cater (KAY-tur)—to provide food for a large group of people

celebrity (sell-EH-bruh-tee)—relating to a famous person

CEO (SEE-EE-OH)—the highest-ranking person in a company; short for chief operating officer

croissant (krwuh-SAHNT)—a crescent-shaped French bread roll made from buttered layers of yeast dough

dignity (DIG-nuh-tee)—a quality that makes people worthy of honor or respect

dot com (DOT KAHM)—an Internet-based company

festivity (fess-TIV-uh-tee)—an activity that is part of a celebration

fortune (FOR-chuhn)—a large amount of money

gender (JEN-dur)—the sex of a person or creature

genetic engineering (juh-NET-ik en-juh-NEER-ing)—inserting genes from one species into another species

inherit (in-HER-it)—to be given someone's property after they die

larva (LAR-vuh)—an insect at the stage of development between an egg and a pupa when it looks like a worm

nourishment (NUR-ish-muhnt)—food that is necessary for growth

paradigm (PA-ruh-dime)—a model

ritual (RICH-oo-uhl)—an action performed as part of a social custom

sensitive (SEN-suh-tiv)—relating to something that should be kept secret

stock option (STOK OP-shuhn)—a benefit a company gives an employee to buy stock in the company at a discount

transport (TRANSS-port)—something that carries someone from one place to another

vegetarian (vej-uh-TER-ee-uhn)—a person who does not eat meat

VISUAL QUESTIONS & WRITING PROMPTS

1. Cyborg and Beast Boy suggest a number of interesting party themes. Think up your own unique party theme and write a paragraph describing what it would include.

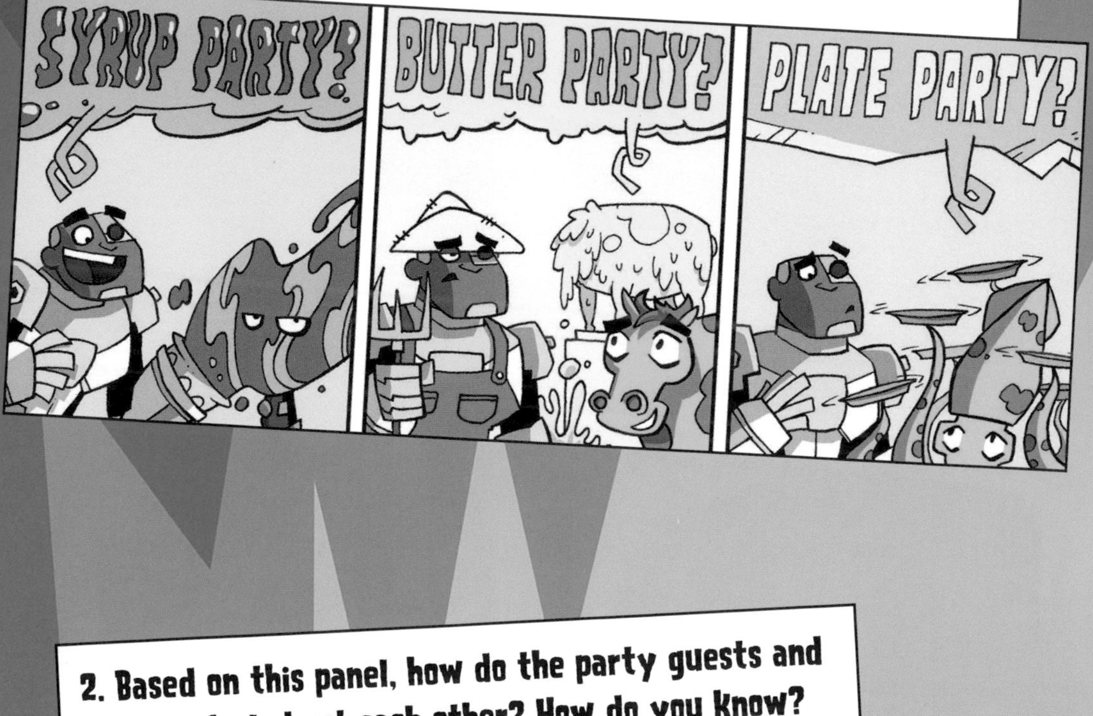

SYRUP PARTY?
BUTTER PARTY?
PLATE PARTY?

2. Based on this panel, how do the party guests and hosts feel about each other? How do you know?

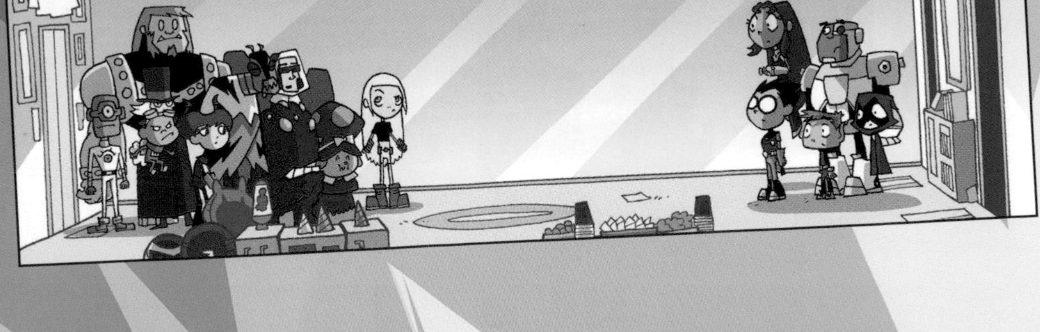

3. Flashbacks help readers understand details from a character's backstory. Based on this flashback, how does Starfire feel about the bathroom at Titan Tower and why?

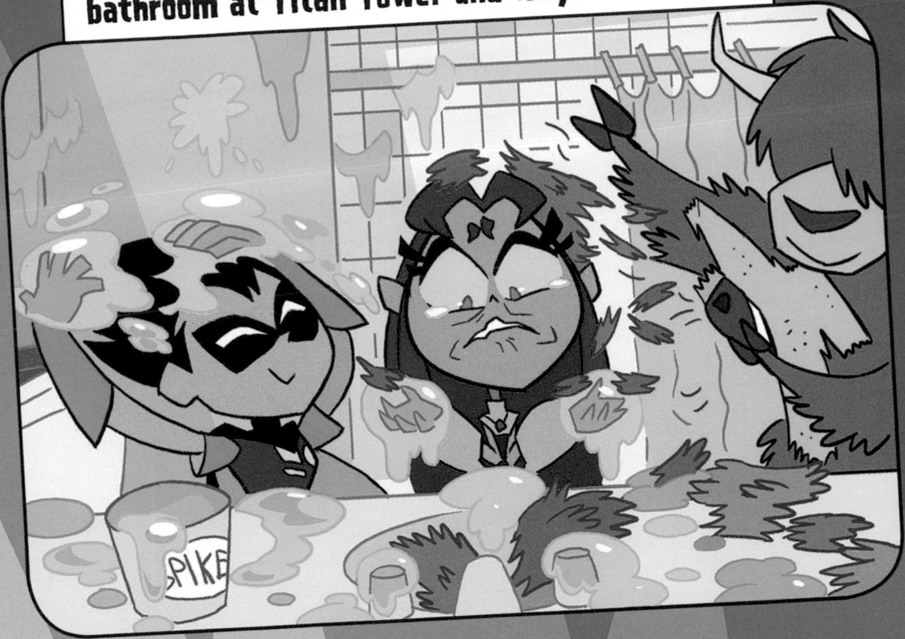
SPIKE

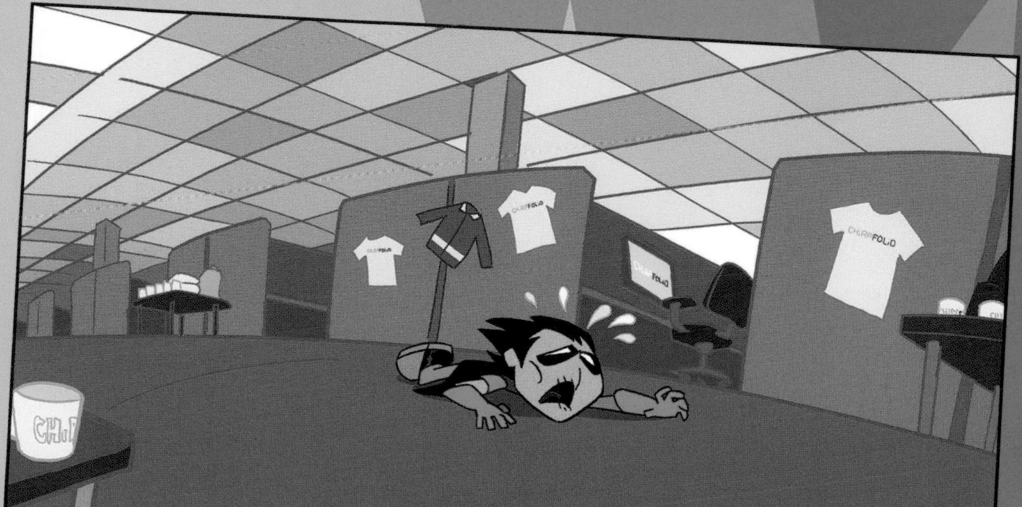

4. What do you think happened to Robin right before this panel? Write a short paragraph describing the events that led him here.

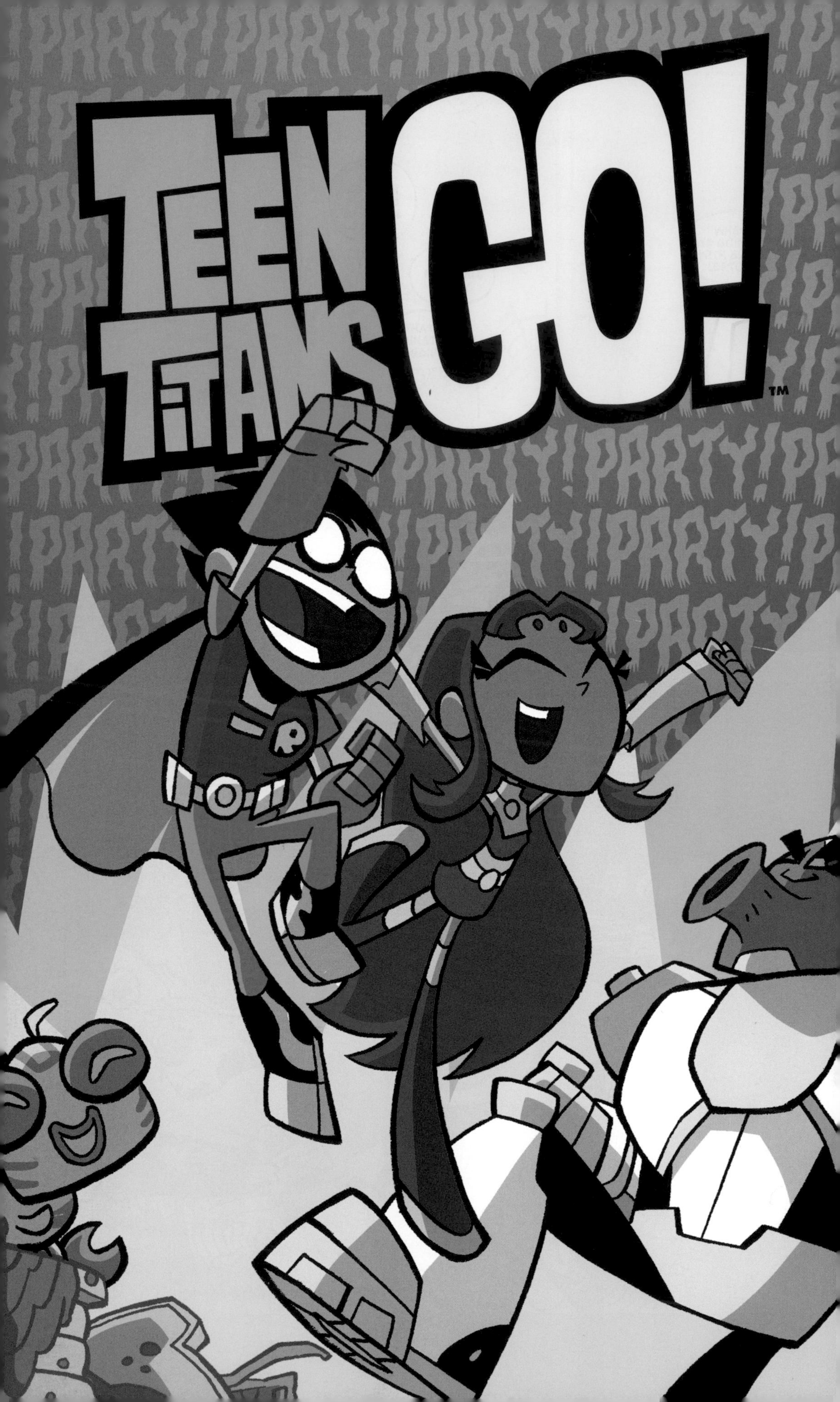
TEEN TITANS GO!™

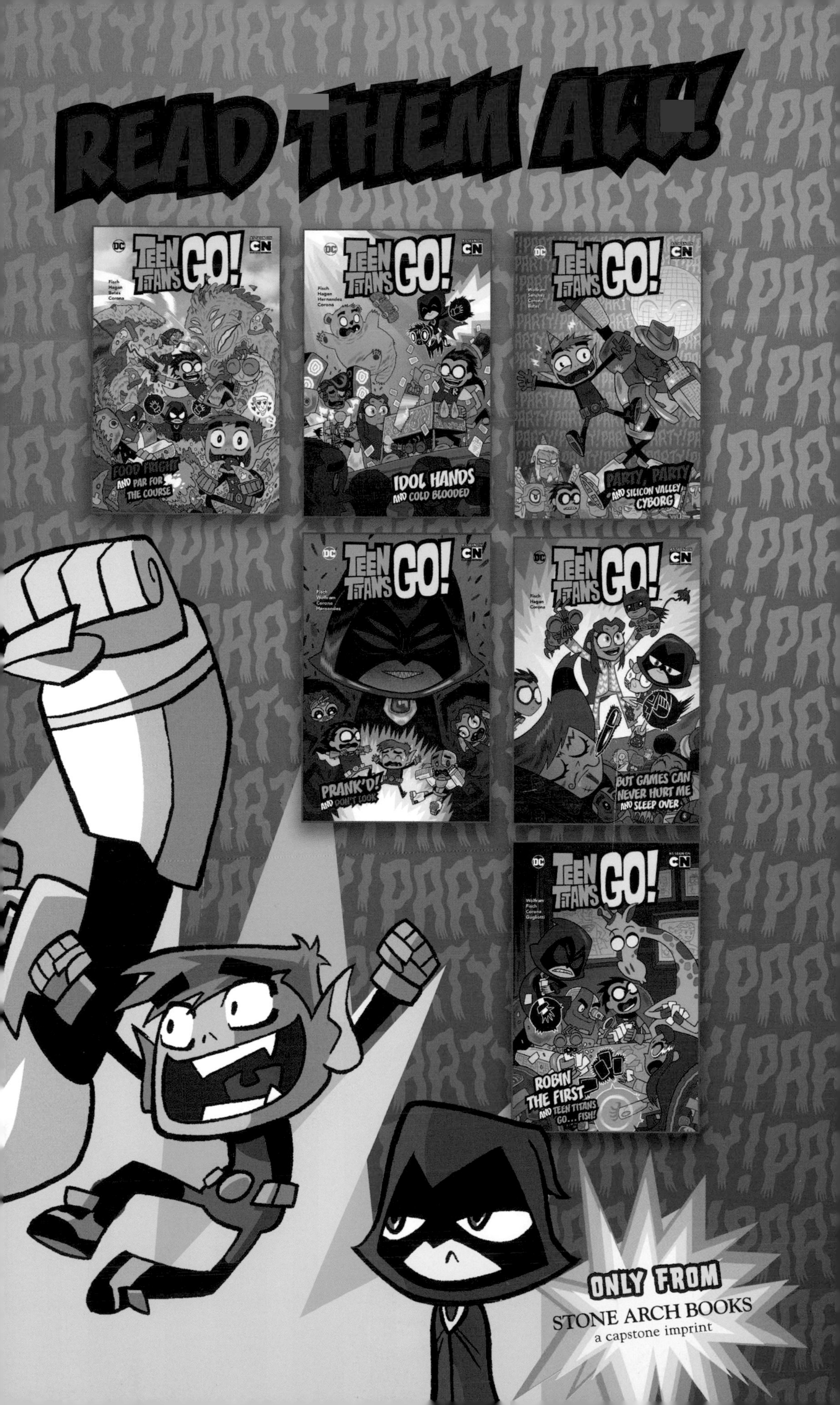
READ 'THEM ALL!
TEEN TITANS GO!
Fisch
Hagan
Bates
Corona
FOOD FRIGHT
AND PAR FOR THE COURSE
TEEN TITANS GO!
Fisch
Hagan
Hernandez
Corona
IDOL HANDS
AND COLD BLOODED
TEEN TITANS GO!
Wolfram
Sanchez
Corona
Bates
PARTY, PARTY
AND SILICON VALLEY CYBORG
TEEN TITANS GO!
Fisch
Wolfram
Corona
Hernandez
PRANK'D!
AND DON'T LOOK
TEEN TITANS GO!
Fisch
Hagan
Corona
BUT GAMES CAN NEVER HURT ME
AND SLEEP OVER
TEEN TITANS GO!
Wolfram
Fisch
Corona
Gugliotti
ROBIN THE FIRST
AND TEEN TITANS GO... FISH!
ONLY FROM
STONE ARCH BOOKS
a capstone imprint

TEEN TITANS GO!™